DARK LEGENDS

JAMIE HAWKE

Editors
Diane Newton
Tracey Byrnes

DARK LEGENDS (this book) is a work of fiction.

WELCOME

Want to never miss a new release, stay up to date on what's going on, and get a silly little spiced-up "Building Your Harem Guide?"

SIGN UP HERE

WARNING: This book contains adult content. A lot!

If you'd like to keep updated on new stories, free-bies, and recommendations of other stories I admire, come check out my FaceBook page at:

https://www.facebook.com/JamieHawkeAuthor.

Thank you for reading!

All the best,

Jamie Hawke

1

Something moved, interrupting my dreams of Red with her peach of an ass pushed up against me, imagining what it would feel like when she was finally ready to go all the way. I'd been just about to slide in, the tip already moving up against her thighs, preparing to find the opening.

Not the best time to interrupt a dream, and not the best dream to interrupt.

Then again, something moved and it was under the sheets. Open air on my cock, something wet around it. Red's pussy?

I opened my eyes, just barely, worried it was still a dream and I'd frighten it away. The sight was confusing at first, until my mind was able to process the image of Pucky there, her horns pointed my way as she bent over my cock, washing it with a cloth from a small Tupperware container of water.

"First time I've been woken up with a cock sponge bath," I said with a laugh, then squirmed as some of the water dripped down to my balls.

She grinned up at me, then lost the smile. "Wait... would it be your first time getting woken up by a blowjob?"

"Yes," I replied, not even having to think about it. As sad as it was, I could count the number of times I'd received blowjobs before meeting these Myths, and that number was definitely less than the number since meeting them. "Though, since I'm awake now, I'm not totally sure this counts."

She arched an eyebrow as she put aside her Tupperware container and towel, then took another, drying first my balls and then my cock.

"Close your eyes," she said.

"What?"

"Just shut up and sleep."

I was about to argue and point out that I was already awake, but realized how totally stupid that would be. Closing my eyes, doing my best to be asleep, I waited.

A gentle caress of a tongue, barely there, met my cock at its base and worked up to just below the tip, then licked across the base of the head. She laughed and I opened my eyes, a shiver running through me.

"Good morning," I said, and then clutched the sheets as she wrapped her mouth around my cock and moved her head down on it—she couldn't quite get all the way, but in good fun mumbled a "Good morning back" with it in there, before pulling back and starting to move a hand along my shaft with her mouth going up and down.

Best way to wake up ever.

It wasn't as action-packed as some of our fun times, me still clearing my head, not fully awake. But for her part, everything was where it needed to be. She had a hand on my balls, massaging them as she ran her other hand along my lower shaft and took the rest in her mouth, bobbing up and down. Her hand twisted with the motion and she took a moment to jerk me off, tongue out as she slid my cock around on it. My chest clenched and I moaned, rocking my hips into the motion as she went back in, wrapping her lips around my tip and then pulling it back into her mouth as she grabbed my ass with both hands and kept moving me, rocking me, as her head moved up and down.

Her horns lit up and an extra level of warmth crept through me, similar to what you get from certain types of massage oil. She came up for air and then took me in both hands for a few strokes, staring at it as if she were creating a work of art and each pump was another act of her creation. When my breathing was hot and heavy, she slowed, went back for the balls, and then took me in her mouth again to finish me off.

Who needed coffee with this to wake up to? As I thrust my hips up and the tingling bliss took hold, my mind rushed through flashbacks of all the images of making love to her and the others since I fell into this crazy adventure. I felt alive, ready to take on the world.

Her eyes were curved with mischief as she took the last drop, swirling her tongue around my tip like an ice cream, watching me.

I didn't move for a long moment, then suddenly sprang up, rolling over to flip Pucky onto her back. "Your turn."

"Are you kidding me?" She swatted my hand away from her pants. "First thing in the morning, I still need a shower. Maybe a candle bath."

"You just did me, so it's my turn."

She guffawed and then shook her head. "You wish you could have my pussy for breakfast. Nope, sorry. I know I'm being selfish but that's how today's going to be."

I laughed, and kissed her, earning a giggle from

her as she squirmed and ran her hands along my chest. "You were sexy as hell, all 'ooh,' and 'ahhh' just now."

"Shut up." I hadn't even realized I'd been making those sounds.

She pulled me in for another kiss, then managed a maneuver that flipped me back, half-boner flapping from side to side and earning another laugh. When she was up and moving for the door, I was about to run after her still nude, when she held out a hand. "Remember where we are."

The grogginess now gone, it hit me. We'd made our way to another safe house, where the last two days since the incident at the convention center had been spent with Myths gathering for the big fight to come. Part of me wanted to relax and make love all day—a large part of me—and maybe paint each other as we'd done in the other house. But we had an immediate goal now, a possible attack incoming any day. We were setting up defenses, pairing up teams based on classes and power levels, and setting up lookouts and scouts.

All this in preparation for King Arthur to come for his sword and, presumably, to try and kill us all. With Morganna's help, of course. Not the real Morganna. Well, kind of... it was all so confusing. Did Riak, taking the power from a dead Morganna for herself, count as her now being the real Morganna? I supposed it did. In a sense, Riak—sister of Pucky—was dead, Morganna having replaced her.

This could also explain why Pucky was acting so giddy and giving. Everyone had their own defense mechanisms. Could wanting to give pleasure to those around her be Pucky's? Not bad for me, but I wanted to be sure she wasn't keeping it all inside.

"If you need someone to talk with," I started, but she gave me a look that said to stop right there.

"My sister went dark a long time ago. Nothing new in this situation, other than her being more of a threat that we need to stop."

I nodded, giving her space, trying to figure out from her expression if this was how she really felt. "Why?" I finally asked.

"Why do they do it?" She waited until I nodded, then explained, "For some it's about power. Some, like Sharon, get kind of taken over. They try to fight it, but unless they have a real connection, like we have, it's hard to fight. I think that's what helped you. You had something to fight for."

That made sense. I could see losing myself if I didn't have these ladies at my side when everything had been going crazy. "And... your sister?"

"Power. She tasted it early on. We both did when

we were sent to the Fae world for training, as many Druids must."

I waited, eyeing her. She had to know that statement needed more story to it.

Finally she sighed, rubbed her hands together, and said, "It's not a big deal, really. This is something Druids do. We have to connect with nature, and that means finding that connection to the spirit world, or the land of the Fae. It also means... temptation."

"In what way?"

She scrunched her nose. "Like an alcoholic, I guess. Well, drugs are a better analogy, because being drunk doesn't really give you power, but in ways certain drugs do. You try a new pill, it makes your mind clear, makes you able to do things you couldn't before... even not feel pain. It's great, right? But not if you get addicted to it, not if you abuse it."

"The shadows... when it had me, I didn't feel like an addict."

"It's not a perfect analogy," she said.

"No, but I get it. There's no... I don't know... rehab for this?"

"As I said, my sister chose this path long ago." Pucky motioned for me to follow her. "Let's get some breakfast and forget about Riak, and focus instead on how to take down Morganna."

I followed, very much aware that those two were

one and the same. But if she was going to be in denial over that fact, I could at least leave it alone for now. When the time came, though, I wasn't about to shoot first and ask questions later. If we could somehow get through to her sister, as I believed was possible after seeing Sharon come to our side, I wanted to ensure that would happen.

"Can we just…" She stopped me in the hallway, turning to grab me by the collar and pull me close, "…focus on the fact that I woke you up with a blowjob?" Her grin was infectious, assisted by the memory of that blowjob. "I think that's enough, no?" I laughed, the bullshit of those dark thoughts fading, and she laughed, nudging me in the side as she added, "But you fucking owe me."

"I'll deliver right here, right now," I said, kneeling and burying my face in her pants, nose nuzzling her.

"Real nice," Elisa said, walking past and patting my head as she went. "If I'd known that was for breakfast, I would've come sooner."

We stumbled out into the kitchen, laughing, my arm around Pucky and Elisa shooting me a wink as she went for the coffee pot. Red was watching something on the tablet in front of her, her back turned to us. We were in a small dining area on the third floor of this safe house over in Arcadia. Not so far from where we'd been, but enough distance to give us space in case there were problems.

I glanced over her shoulder and saw news coverage of what they were calling the 'convention center riots', making it look like some conservative group had protested about a group of women who'd dressed like super-sexy versions of the Ex Gods characters, like in the movies but even sluttier.

Watching through the screen, we saw the version the normies saw—people yelling at each other, a fight breaking out, and it leading to chaos. To be fair, the Ex Gods cosplayers had done a damn fine job, and the one who had the sides of her pink hair shaved to look like Threed was practically naked, showing off hot body tattoos that I had to think might be real. If they'd put those kind of costumes on the actors in the movies, I would've seen it in the theater way more times than the two I did.

"Damn," I said, as a Jehovah's-witness kind of guy ran up and clocked a man with a shaved head across the jaw, and then the woman painted blue like Andromida from Ex Gods came in with a knee to the balls and elbow to the throat. That's when it got nasty.

Red glanced up and grinned. Her lip piercing sparkled, standing out against her black lipstick.

"Finally you're up," Red said.

"He *was*," Pucky cut in, handing me a scone and biting back a laugh. "Not anymore."

"Subtle," Red said with a roll of her eyes.

"But whenever it's just us in a room, isn't that how it goes?" Elisa said, joining us to watch the footage.

"I've watched it at least five times," Red said.

"Yeah, it's interesting," I said, biting into one of the scones.

"Sure, but I'm just trying to figure out how the Threed wannabe gets her ass so sculpted. I mean, look there." She paused it, holding up the screen for me to see while zooming in on the lady's ass. "Isn't that hot?"

"Trick question," I said, not taking the bait. "When it comes to asses, you all have the best of 'em."

She frowned and closed the app.

"But…" Elisa nodded to the door. "Sharon's already out there training, the others probably are too.

"No sign of Arthur yet, I take it." I sipped the coffee she handed me, taking a moment to treasure the perfect mix of creamer and coffee, no sugar.

"If he'd come, we'd know, even with the defenses Mowgli set up. They're strong, but Morganna," she consciously didn't look at Pucky as she said it, "combined with the power of Arthur? It's going to be a real battle, one we won't win easily. Which is why we need to get you trained up on this Tempest business. It's getting late in the day already."

I broke my scone in two and ate my half in two bites, nodding as crumbs fell down my shirt. With a quick sip of the coffee, I said, "Ready and excited."

"Let's go learn how to use Excalibur properly, then."

2

W hat made training as a Tempest hard, they explained to me, was that there simply weren't many of us around. Only a Protector could choose a class, while most Myths and Legends were born into theirs. The exceptions were those who took over as former Myths or Legends, such as Riak with Morganna. In theory, that could lead to a class change, but this was rare.

And from all of that, Tempests weren't easily found. Overseas there were more, Mowgli explained, such as in China and Japan. There was the Little Mermaid, but she had sworn off fighting years ago and, while technically on our side, wouldn't be any help here.

They got me into the penthouse, a suite that was

cleared out for this specific purpose, and Pucky had Excalibur waiting for me.

"We're going to train with real blades?" I asked.

Red stood with Elisa on the opposite side of the room, drawing her sword—much thinner and shorter, but still very much a sword. "Would you jump into the ocean only having tried swimming without water?"

Red held a sword at the ready. I glanced at Elisa nervously.

"We've enchanted the room to ensure there will be no death or maiming," she assured me. "Cuts though… we'll see."

"We'll see?" I questioned, not liking the sound of that.

Not that it mattered, though, because Red was already darting toward me, red cloak billowing out behind her so that it was like a tidal wave of blood sweeping in. I took a step back and held up my sword, not sure how I was supposed to be doing anything different here than a warrior would do. When she struck, I parried, but she was too fast, coming back around to slap me in the ass with the flat of her blade before dancing off to prepare for another strike.

Damn, that stung.

"Hmm," Elisa said, shaking her head. "I was hoping that it was going to come naturally."

"What was?" I asked.

"The Tempest powers. Maybe..." She held a hand up to Red. "You're too much in your head. Get out of there, focus here." She touched her stomach, her sexy, revealed abs. Yeah, I could focus there no problem. Her finger turned back to me. "Not mine, yours."

"Sure, focus on my abs." I nodded, knowing that wasn't what she meant but unable to grasp what she was going for.

Somehow my new powers were supposed to take over, but only if I let them. Problem was, I had no idea what that meant in a practical sense. When Elisa lowered her hand and Red came at me again, I felt like an idiot swinging my sword without any magic or energy flowing from my stomach. Red's strike nearly hit me but I stepped back defensively and my shield—a level two warrior upgrade—burst into effect, deflecting her strike. What a relief to know it still worked, even though I'd switched away from being a warrior.

Another strike and somehow she was behind me, this time giving me a swift kick in the ass.

"Going to have to do better than that," Red said,

pulling back and out of the way of my strike. Seeing that I'd overextended myself, she came back in and hit me with her shoulder against my ribcage, knocking me off balance—and she'd gotten her foot behind mine, so that I tripped and dropped my sword.

A flash of magic hit me and I rolled sideways, narrowly avoiding falling onto my blade. Damn, that was close.

"See, the protection charm works," Elisa said, looking relieved. I laughed nervously and pushed myself up to fight some more.

"I just don't get it," I admitted.

"Imagine you're one with the universe, one with more than nature, but the elements. The air you breathe, the water in your body, and more. Embrace it."

My frown made it clear what I thought of this, but I tried again… and got my butt kicked again. None of this was coming as easily as I wanted it to. Being a warrior made sense to me, but being one with the water, flowing and attacking like a wave? Fuck all that. Every time I'd played games like Final Fantasy I'd gone warrior. I knew how to hack and slash, what it meant to charge in with a roar and slice my enemies in two.

Another attack came and I did my best to focus on the flow, to feel it and move as they'd told me, but in the end I reverted to my instincts, slamming Red's sword aside and making a strike that she parried and darted away from.

"You're still not focused," Elisa said.

She was right. My mind was on the fact that I wasn't seeing my family, and everything that had happened since I'd become a Protector. I'd fucking killed my childhood hero—Peter Pan! That shit wasn't right.

To make it all worse, it was confusing. I was a Protector, in training to learn how to help protect the Myths from my own government. Essentially, they'd stabbed me with some magic blade that made it official, and now I was more on their side than humanity's. What did that make me? Some sort of enemy of the people, and yet… how often had a large group or government persecuted others who didn't deserve it? They didn't understand these Myths, not like I did.

Except I really barely knew them at all. Hence the confusion.

"Let's give Sharon a turn," Elisa said, motioning Red out of there. "Let him get more experience against a Legend."

"Ex-Legend," Sharon growled, approaching me with claws at the ready. Why was it that the moment I saw her hands, I imagined myself back on that stairwell, her hand on my cock? I gulped, trying to focus, trying to clear my mind, and then she came at me.

For at least a split second, I felt that connection to something bigger than myself. It was almost like before with going into the Fae world and the sensation I'd felt when taking Excalibur to be mine, and I moved with grace and precision. Only, it faltered and I stumbled, the blade hitting magic as it nearly sliced at Sharon's neck.

She pulled back from that, eyes narrowed with anger, and slashed at my back, tearing my clothes.

"Fuck," I said, recovering to try again.

"You trying to kill me?" she asked.

"All I'm trying to do is learn," I insisted.

She nodded, took a deep breath, and repositioned herself for an attack.

"You got this!" Pucky called out from the doorway to the balcony, where I only now realized she'd stepped out for a bit. That sounded like a great plan at the moment. Clearing my head with some fresh air, not putting up with this futile endeavor.

But Sharon was prowling, preparing to strike, and I had no choice but to keep training, keep trying. I wasn't about to look like a quitter in front of my team. My sword thrust out at Sharon's side and she pulled back, and without warning Red came in again, slashing for my arms with her sword.

The magic hit and we were both sent stumbling back. When my head cleared, I came to the realization that we weren't approaching this correctly.

"How am I going to stand a chance against Arthur and Morganna?" I asked, lowering my sword and turning on Elisa. "This is ridiculous."

"The how is easy—though the fight won't be. You have us." She gestured for Sharon to attack, but I didn't raise my sword.

Not that Sharon cared, apparently. She moved toward me, transforming as she did. No longer was she a petite, crazy-looking lady. Instead, a werewolf stared back at me with glowing red eyes, claws at the ready, and teeth gnashing.

Her advance didn't catch me off guard, but I was thrown by the way seeing her took me back to the convention center, to Chris. My best friend... and he'd betrayed me. I slashed out, catching her along the arm and drawing blood, and she growled, knocking me back.

"I'm sor..." I started to apologize, but she plowed into me again, the cut already starting to heal. Badass.

Again I swung, this time wanting to test her. I was careful not to go for any lethal strikes, but part of the reason they'd put me up against her was that she could handle it. And, apparently, heal.

Sharon wasn't the same Big Bad Wolf as the original, but I started wondering if there could be any truth to cutting open the wolf's stomach like in the fairy tale, and it living—seeing as in wolf form Sharon could heal herself. Trying to figure out what was real from those stories and what wasn't was a mind fuck in itself, but I was starting to see the hints of what made sense.

She snarled and again I was reminded of Chris's betrayal. I cursed as I swung my sword, trying to pull on the spirit of water, the flow of the power in this sword, but instead Sharon slammed the blade out of the way, claws going for my throat, and she had me.

I tried rolling with it, but she controlled herself, glow fading from her eyes as she flipped me over and let me fall, my sword clattering away.

Pinning me there like that, she leaned in close and said, "We've been here before, no?"

The image of her on the stairwell at the Con flashed into my mind, the memory of her grabbing my dick, and I felt a nudge of blood flow down below. She winked, but I flipped her off of me and recovered before Mr. Boner came out to play.

"Won't happen again," I said, charging her for a takedown.

She easily spun with it, slamming me to the ground. I groaned, got up, and went at it again. Slam. My breath left my lungs and I lay there gasping.

After the third time she knocked me on my ass, I stood and kicked Excalibur's handle, cursing. But it wasn't the fight or losing that bothered me, and she could tell. Transforming back to normal, she followed me out of the training room and to the walkway nearby that looked out over what appeared to be an old manufacturing room, with various machine parts and conveyer belts.

"You're not doing so bad in there," she said, standing next to me. I couldn't help but notice that her fingers were bleeding at the nails, where her claws had grown from, but were quickly healing.

"I don't... I mean, at least you all are here with me, but..."

"This is about your friend?" When I nodded, she continued. "It wasn't his fault. They had his family. And besides, he only gave you up to me, and I like to think maybe he saw something in me that made doing so less of an issue. Maybe he saw that I didn't really want to hurt you."

My gut said to trust her, the side of me that had dealt with the shadows after her bite. Part of me felt a connection, though maybe it was a dark connection—I couldn't be sure. Was I supposed to embrace this kinship, or blame her for nearly turning me into a creature of the night? I had no idea, but knew there was way too much going on in my head to decide right now.

For one, I couldn't forget the way she'd been on the stairwell that first night we'd met, when she'd tackled me and managed to fight the darkness when grabbing my cock. A weird way to fight evil, considering all the church's views on such matters. I'd since mentioned it to Elisa, who assured me it had to do with intimacy and a human connection. When Sharon could make that bond, she could fight the evil influence of the Fae world.

A glance over at Sharon showed she might've been remembering that same moment, because her hand was gripping the cylindrical railing, finger moving along it, as her eyes moved along my crotch.

I cleared my throat. She blinked, saw that I'd caught her, and then turned away—but not before I saw the rosy blush spreading across her face.

"I'm trying to understand," I said in an attempt to bring the topic back to Chris and his betrayal. "But… Oh, shit."

"What?" she asked.

"His family, are they…?"

She faced me, embarrassment turning to worry. "You can't go after them. Not when we're here setting this trap for Arthur and Morganna. Not when they've done so much for you."

"You don't think they'd let me go?"

"They'd be stupid to!"

I processed that, feeling my chest start to heave and my fingers growing twitchy. "And Chris?" She looked away, even started to turn, but my hand shot out and grabbed her by the wrist. "Sharon... tell me what you know."

"All I know is how the Legends are," she muttered, eyes on my hand touching her, an instant calm seeming to take over. For a moment, she hesitated, then put her free hand on top of mine and stared intently into my eyes. "In my mind he was free to go, but I arranged all that... when they find out they can leverage him, which they likely already have, they'll go after him. Kill him to teach you a lesson? Maybe. Hold him to lure you into doing something stupid? More likely."

"Then you're getting me out of here, and showing me where he is."

"Don't let them bait you."

"If his life might be on the line?" I stood tall, determined. "I have no choice."

3

"Jack…" Sharon's eyes were wide, pleading, but as cute as that was there was no way it would work on me. "You want to leave here with me, the woman who tried to kill you as far as you know? The woman who was your enemy only two days ago?"

She made good points, but they didn't negate the need. "Of course not. We'll bring the team."

"Where?" Red asked, stepping up to join us, giving me an awkward smile.

"He wants to go after his friend." Sharon folded her arms and started to smile, as if that was enough to get Red on her side, and in doing so would change my mind.

"And you know where he'd be held if they had

him," Red said, looking at Sharon with a new level of interest.

"What?"

"Yes, this is good." Red glanced around and saw Pucky and Elisa returning from taking a bathroom break. "Hey, ladies. Sharon has a good idea."

"What?" Sharon looked lost—the deer staring into the headlights. "No, I…" Seeing the expressions of interest and excitement on Elisa and Pucky's faces, the Big Bad Wolf deflated, giving in. "We go back to the hideout, the one I know all about, and make sure they're not holding Jack's friend. If they are, free him, of course."

"Better than sticking around here!" Pucky exclaimed.

Elisa, however, looked a little less sure. "We have a lot of training for you," she said to me. "The sword, your new class—"

"Would both be better utilized against a real enemy," I countered. "Imagine, me getting my levels up out there, grinding, refocusing my skill trees on the Tempest branch."

"He makes a good argument," Pucky said.

"And either way, I'm not about to leave Chris stranded. He might be a prick sometimes, but that prick is still my best friend."

"You're not going alone," Elisa said. "And we're not going without telling Mowgli."

"But what if he doesn't let—"

"No," she interrupted me. "I said 'tell' not ask. If this is important, it has to be done."

"Just like that?"

Red glanced over at Elisa, then rolled her eyes and leaned into me, conspiratorially. "The thing with her is… she believes that everything in the universe has a purpose, and a reason. So if you feel this kind of conviction, not only does she want to do it for you, but because she believes the universe must be saying it's the right move."

"And to ignore that," Elisa whispered as if it was a very holy topic, "could risk the wrath of the universe."

I smiled as if she was joking, but quickly saw that she wasn't.

"Oh, right. But that all means we're doing it, right?"

"Of course," Red said with a chuckle.

"Doing what?" Pucky asked.

"Going to save his friend," Sharon said, not looking happy about it at all. It wasn't like I could blame her. "Chris."

Pucky frowned, glanced around, and then shrugged. "Fucking awesome. I was getting bored here anyway. I'll go tell Mowgli." She jogged off as both Elisa and I opened our mouths to stop her, knowing she wouldn't be handling it tactfully at all. Neither of us followed through, though, because this way was much easier.

"Let's head for the doors," Elisa said. "I'll call the car."

"Not a way we can back out?" Sharon asked.

Red grunted. "You can stay, if you don't want to be part of the team."

Sharon followed without another word.

We were already at the door, passing by the guards, when a bashful-looking Pucky and an angry Mowgli caught up with us.

"Whose brilliant plan is this?" Mowgli asked.

I meekly raised a hand.

"You do realize this whole situation is set up around you?" he asked. "If you're not here, we have no trap, we have no reason for Arthur to come."

"No bait, you mean," I countered, even though I was perfectly fine with being the bait. I was more annoyed that he was even trying to argue this.

"We're going to be fast," Elisa said. "Don't worry."

His mouth fell open, then he laughed. "If Elisa's on board, I know there's no talking you out of it." He glanced around, lowering his voice. "But at least go out the back way. For one, I don't need everyone questioning why you're not here. And two, for all we know the enemy might have eyes on us at this point. Keep a low profile." Then he reached into his pocket and handed me a small green stone that vibrated gently when I took it. "Use this to call for help if needed."

We agreed, and moved back toward the rear exit while Mowgli had a car go around to meet us. As pissed as I was at Chris, what he'd done made some sort of sense. Maybe I would've done the same in his situation. Probably not—I would've gone after whoever had threatened my parents and seen them punished. At least, the new me would.

For now, I would simply focus on the fact that I had a friend who was in trouble, and I was on my way to save him.

The driver followed Sharon's instructions of where to go, from her position in the front passenger seat as we threaded our way through lines of city traffic onto a highway where the traffic was barely moving, before it cleared and we were off again.

"Having fun?" Pucky asked out of nowhere.

"In general, or right at this moment?"

"I mean with all this—it's like nonstop action, no? Obviously not when we're stuck in traffic, but you know, fighting, fucking... fighting, fucking...

It's kind of our thing." She grinned, then blew me a kiss.

Elisa laughed, while Sharon looked at me with a seductive curiosity. Red, as always, tried to look uninterested but was glancing my way out of the corner of her eyes.

"You're asking me if I like fucking and kicking the ass of bad guys?" I laughed, not really sure how to answer that except to say, "Fuck yes."

"Thought so." She shrugged. "I honestly can't see how anyone would want to spend their life behind a desk, or out working construction or something. I mean, those are both great, for people who need to make a living. But give me fucking and fighting any day. Only fucking you, of course, and only fighting the bad guys."

"Of course," Elisa said with a grin. "I imagine the whole part about risking their lives would turn off most people from this lifestyle, but…"

She cocked her head, unfolding her legs and then folding them in a way that gave me a perfect view of downstairs—no panties, apparently.

"You've seen *Basic Instinct*, I take it?" I said after taking a heavy breath.

She shrugged. "You know, I was starting to think I didn't get all your references and obsessions, so…

figured why not. Couldn't sleep, and it was on some list of great movies."

"What happened?" Sharon asked from the front seat, apparently having not seen, but I didn't say anything. Elisa only smiled at me.

"Well, I'm ready for action of every sort," Pucky said, changing the topic. She was at my side so she could've seen the show Elisa gave me, but I wasn't sure.

"In here?" Elisa asked, glancing around.

I chuckled, thinking she was joking, then adjusted in my seat when her expression became serious. "Honestly, I might need a bit of a break…" I hated to admit it, but was pretty sure my dick was swollen and anything involving the little guy at the moment would hurt as much as it would feel good.

She frowned. "I'll just have to take it out on the enemy then. With fighting, though, to be clear."

"We've got time," Red said. "Just… don't let the driver see you." She must've noticed my look of confusion, because she added a circling motion with her finger, then pointed at Elisa. "Don't be selfish. Help her out."

"That's not necessary," Elisa said, but her eyes were looking at me with anticipation.

Hell, they'd helped me out plenty of times, and if she was feeling the need enough so that she'd watched the movie and not worn panties, I was happy to do my part.

"We don't want you getting distracted in there," I said, repositioning so that I could reach over with my left arm, hoping Sharon and the driver wouldn't notice. Red and Pucky both watched, eyes following my hand as it slid up Elisa's thigh. She uncrossed her legs and my hand caressed her, feeling how moist she was, and then I slid a finger in.

She bit her lip to stop from moaning, moving her hips with the motion as I started fingering her, then went for the clit.

"Everyone okay back there?" Sharon asked, glancing back.

"Yeah, just... imagining the fight," Pucky said, glancing up and trying to look innocent. "You know, mental preparation and all."

"Yeah, we're totally the meditation types," Red said with a scoff, eyes not leaving my hand as my middle finger caressed Elisa. "Not you?"

"Oh, it's... something I could try," Sharon replied, turning back to watch the road. The driver, at least, kept driving. No comment, even if he did notice something.

"Maybe we should try humming as a mantra?" Pucky said, and winked at me. A glance over at Elisa showed why—she was clutching the seat, trying her best not to make a sound.

"Oh, yeah," I said. "Something like that? Oh yeah, oh yeah?"

Pucky chuckled, eyes sparkling. "Of course. That's the one I taught you, right? Imagine you're slaughtering Shades, kicking back those bastard Legends, and each time you land a strike, it's 'Oh, yeah!'"

"With us, Sharon?" Red asked, actually amused now.

"Really, you all do this before fights?" Sharon asked.

"Sure," Pucky replied, earning her a skeptical glance over his glasses from the driver, but he went back to driving.

"Here we go, with me," Pucky said, and we all joined in as she said, "Oh yeah, oh yeah, oh yeah!"

Elisa was the loudest, as you would guess, and as I really felt the hardness of her clit, a squirt too that we'd have to clean up later, she hit the roof and nearly screamed, "Oh, yes!"

The rest of us were laughing. When Sharon turned back in confusion, my hand was back on my lap. Elisa was breathing deep, smiling wide.

"Really great meditation," Elisa said. "I fucking destroyed them in my mind."

"Yeah, I'll have to try it your way on the way back," Red said.

Pucky laughed. "You and me both, girl."

Sharon frowned, shook her head, and turned around again. "You all have weird ways. Not sure I'm there yet."

I bit back a laugh, and reached over again to caress Elisa, but she squirmed away, then kissed me on the cheek before whispering in my ear, "It's sensitive now, thanks to you." She kissed my neck, then leaned back, reclining her head and closing her eyes.

A few minutes later Red said, "Seriously, fucking driving. I'm ready to bash some skulls together."

"Aren't you always?" Pucky asked.

"What, I seem tense to you?"

"You do to me," I admitted. "Any reason for that?"

Elisa opened her eyes at this and said, "I know… She's not used to holding out like this."

"And she doesn't have to," Pucky pointed out.

Red frowned. "Changing topic. Focus on fighting bad guys, not my sexual decisions."

Naturally, I wanted to stay on the subject of sex with her, but Elisa was frowning now, glancing up at Sharon. She leaned forward, whispering, "We have to remember that she's only been with us a couple days. For all we know, this could be a trap."

"She was trying to fight it before," I countered.

"Even the first time I met her, when she bit me. There was some of this version of her in there, I saw it when she touched my..." My voice trailed off, as I wasn't sure where to go with it from there.

Pucky looked amused, Elisa confused, and Red frowned.

"Touched your what?" Elisa asked.

A silence filled the car, broken only by Sharon as she turned back and said, "His penis."

"Oh?"

"It was hanging out there, a weird moment. And by the way, wolf, remember? We have excellent hearing."

"Elisa was just saying we're not sure if we should trust you," Red said, and laughed. "But hey, if you've already gotten to... what base is grabbing a guy's penis, anyway? Well, whatever base that is, I guess you're one of us."

"Can we stop talking about my... penis?" I said, embarrassed that they were talking about it at all, but even more so that they made it sound so medical.

"I'd heard that happened," Red admitted. "Honestly, it made me wonder what kind of guy you were, running around in hotel stairwells with your *penis* out." She clearly had noticed that referring to it as such annoyed me.

"It's not a habit of mine," I protested. "She attacked me in the bathroom, while I was finishing up a piss. I just couldn't get it back in before getting out of there—wait, no, I did but was wearing boxers and couldn't get my pants up. It sort of flopped out of the flap and... one thing led to another."

Pucky was the first to laugh. "I can't imagine..." She broke into peals of laughter again, this time hitting the seat next to her, and soon Elisa was chuckling beside her, Red grinning. "Holy shit, and what, Sharon, you just saw a penis there and grabbed it?"

Sharon frowned, trying to remember. "It was like I felt it against my ass first, growing, and even that little bit of closeness pulled me from the shadow. Imagine being in a pool, drowning, and you see a way out—a railing or flotation device—you grab at it, right?"

"So his *penis* was your flotation device?" That made Pucky crack up even more.

"Actually, yeah, in a strange way." Sharon chuckled now too. Even the driver was likely glancing my way in the rearview mirror, I imagined, but couldn't tell for certain because of his shades.

"Ladies..." I protested.

"And then we kissed," Sharon added, her laughter fading as she took on a far-off look for a moment before turning her gaze my way with a curious way of assessing me.

"You… kissed?" Pucky asked, her laughter gone now too, turning to me. "Wow, you had an action-packed weekend at the Con."

"It happened," I admitted.

"So if you think about it," Red said, looking very humored now, "Sharon here was the first of all of us to get into his pants."

I opened my mouth to protest, but yeah, it was kinda true. Not in the same way, at all, but still.

Sharon caught the awkwardness and turned around, giving the driver a direction, and we all drove in silence for a bit.

"Is it that big of a deal?" I asked.

Pucky scrunched her face, then shook her head. "No. Shouldn't be."

"You have to understand, she was a Legend," Elisa added as if explaining something simple to a child.

"Grasping for her flotation device," I noted.

Elisa nodded, conceding that point.

"And I had no reason to stop her," I added. "I mean, it'd been a while before that."

"Which is one of the problems," Pucky countered. "If you were just in a state where you'd let anyone grab your dick, it feels less special that you let me."

I laughed. "No offense, but I'd just met you and

was running for my life. You jacked me off to calm me down."

"You did what?" Red asked with an incredulous scoff.

"I…" Pucky blushed, face in her hands.

"Sorry," I added. "I'm just saying, what we have now is special. Those first few hours of chaos and confusion became great real fast, but I don't know of many guys who would've called a time out in the moment."

"He makes a good point," Red said.

Pucky sighed. "I know." Turning to me, she added, "And now? You're in the same situation, let's say. Fucking Goldilocks herself offers to wrap her sweet lips around your huge cock… What do you do?"

I'd almost forgotten about Goldilocks, but the mention of her here piqued my curiosity. There seemed to be a real version of pretty much every character I'd ever heard of, and I made a note to myself to remember to ask about Santa Claus and the others like him. As for her answer, of course I said, "I'd tell her I'm with you all."

"With us all…" Elisa let the words linger, then bit her lip to stop from laughing.

"Is there a better way to put it?" I asked.

"No," Red answered. "That sounds about right. And that's the issue, isn't it. We've confused you."

"How so?" Pucky asked.

"Don't you see, he doesn't know what his romantic, or sexual, or whatever situation is."

Pucky shrugged. "Why the fuck not? It's simple—he's with us."

"I think what she means," Elisa said, "is in our eyes, we're your team. Anyone on the team is fair game—and part of our little situation here. You say yes, and we like them enough to let them be an insider to begin with, it only strengthens our bond to keep them as involved as possible."

I gulped, not sure what to make of this.

"Right," Red said, but then a wicked grin crossed her face. "And on that note… isn't Sharon pretty much part of the team now?"

Sharon turned back at that, curious, waiting. I had to admit, the question piqued my interest as well.

"Er," was all Pucky could get out.

"Tell you what," Elisa said, seeming to really be considering this. "Sharon, prove yourself on this mission, show us you've really turned over a new leaf… and I think that'll be the first discussion we all have when we're on our way out of there."

"So it's an audition to see if I get to join you all in

playing with his cock?" she asked, and even the driver had to laugh at that.

"I didn't mean it like that," Elisa said. "And this is all assuming you want to be part of the team—being on the team certainly doesn't mean you *have* to fool around with any of us, and it doesn't obligate him to put out—"

"Thanks," I said, chuckling in the awkwardness.

She gave me a nod. "I didn't mean it to come out that way. But being on the team means you're one of us, and we'd treat you as such. From there, it's all about what happens, what you want to happen, and what comes naturally."

Sharon bit her lip, nodding at that. "I'd like to be part of the team, on those conditions."

"Good, then let's rescue this Chris guy and get the hell back to the safe house," Red said, though there was a look of hesitation in her eyes when she glanced Sharon's way. Of course, I'd nearly forgotten —Red Riding Hood and the Big Bad Wolf, on one team? Possibly even sharing a man, if it came to that? I'd have to check in with her when we had a moment alone again to ask how she really felt about this. If she wasn't okay with it, I had to say I wouldn't be either.

"Seconded," Pucky added, apparently having given the whole idea some thought. "Personally, I like the idea of having someone crazier than myself on the team. Makes me seem more normal."

"Ha," Sharon said sarcastically. "As much as I'm dreading this, all the awkward talk… makes me almost glad to say we're there, we've arrived."

"It's all relative," I said, agreeing completely. The idea of risking our lives in a fight against evil fairy tales sounded like just the thing to get my mind off of that discussion.

4

We had pulled up to what looked like a community college. Sharon was already moving for the door when Red leaned over the seat and grabbed her arm.

"Here?"

"Where else?" Sharon shrugged. "It's not a base, but was one of the fallback points I heard discussed. The most likely place they would've taken Chris."

"Why's that?" I asked.

"Large area, public enough where they know we'd prefer not to make a scene," Elisa said. "I'm guessing here. But… what I'm just realizing for the first time, Sharon, is how you can be so much more useful to us."

"Intel?" Pucky said, sitting up straight and grinning in Sharon's direction. "She's right."

Red guffawed.

"Still not sure you can trust me?" Sharon asked, glancing down at Red's hand still on her wrist, then slowly working her way out of the grip. "Well maybe after this, you'll know you can."

"I hope so," Red replied, and then we were all piling out of the car and into the community college parking lot.

"We'll want to go in through the art wing," Sharon said, indicating a route between several tall, white buildings to our right. Palm trees stood tall, lining the path in a way that made me feel very Californian, a point that reminded me why we were here to begin with. Chris needed my help.

Sharon took the lead, though when we reached the first tree, she paused, looking me up and down, and then turning to Elisa. "I have an idea."

"Being?" she asked.

"We haven't tried it yet," Sharon glanced around, "and can't out here. But... Jack has changed before... right? Into a wolf, I mean."

I frowned, not liking where this was going.

"He did," Elisa replied. "And lost control, almost."

"Almost." Sharon grinned. "If you all... Yes, even you, Red, can try and trust me for this, I think we can make it work."

"Make what work, exactly?" Pucky asked.

"I can stroll in there as a wolf, with Jack here at my side… also as a wolf. They'll think we belong, that we're—"

"Hell no," Red said, voice rising enough to earn us some looks from several young college kids passing. An older woman followed and I thought it might be their mother, but then remembered we were at a community college and she could just as well be their classmate.

"You think she'd make a move on Jack?" Pucky asked, seemingly not committed either way.

"She'd be leading him into a trap. Think about it —him letting in the shadows, surrounded by Legends. It's setting up the Protector for a fall, plain and simple."

"Or it's me trying to help in the best way I know how," Sharon spat back. "You'd rather we all run in with weapons blazing?"

"We've faced greater foes than whatever's in there waiting for us," Red replied.

"But better not to if it's not necessary," Elisa said. "And I sense something in Sharon that maybe you don't see."

Sharon gave her a very appreciative look, then turned to Red. "I know you've had a history with me… and whoever was before me. I get that—but who here hasn't ever been tempted by the shadows?

They took over, and I lost the fight. But not anymore, okay? I'm doing everything I can to ensure that never happens again, and you have my word, for whatever that's worth to you, that this isn't a trap. This is just me, standing here trying to help."

Red glared, seeming madder at this than if the lady had attacked her.

"Let the wolfie help," Pucky said, half teasing it seemed, but also genuine. "Come on."

"You're sure about her?" Red asked Elisa.

Elisa considered her, then walked up to Sharon and held a hand up to her face, white light taking on the form of a swan and emerging, wings spread wide, and then floated into Sharon.

"There you go," Elisa said, turning back to Red. "Now even if the shadow attempts a takeover, she'll have a part of me with her to help fight it."

Red blinked, confused, but nodded.

"How… exactly, does that work?" Sharon looked shaken.

"It's nothing, really," Elisa replied. "But if you feel you need my help, say so. You'll feel a warmth, and I'll work from out here to walk you through whatever's happening."

Sharon ran a hand through her wild hair, nodded, and then turned to me. "So we're doing this?"

"Do I need to worry about the wolf taking over?" I asked, turning from her to Elisa, then Red. "I mean, is that a concern?"

"My thought is that you're tied to her, in that sense," Elisa replied. "If she doesn't cave, neither should you. But more than that, you are a Tempest now. Tempests actually have a much stronger ability to fight the shadows, as light falls within their powers."

"It didn't work for King Arthur," I pointed out.

"Stronger ability, not perfect."

I nodded, gulped, and said, "I'll take those odds."

"Be careful," Pucky said, giving me a quick hug, and a peck on the cheek. I never knew how to act around these women in situations like this. Was I supposed to give each of them a hug and a kiss, to avoid any jealousy? Or was it not like a series of relationships, but more like a team that bonded in the bedroom? Judging by the way neither Red nor Elisa seemed to care, I took the gamble that it was more of the latter, though took two looks back at each of them to be sure.

Apparently, I'd been too obvious in my hesitation, as Elisa laughed, shaking her head at me. "Don't worry. If I'm feeling needy I'll be sure you give me a quickie before you go. You'll be fine in there."

I frowned, and Red frowned back, though I

wasn't sure if she was teasing me or not. There was a hint of humor in her eyes.

"Whatever," I said, turning to Sharon. "How do we do this?"

"She read minds or something?" Sharon asked in a whisper.

"I'm starting to wonder."

"Right…" Sharon gave Elisa a worried glance, then said, "if she's right about your transformation being linked to mine, it should be easy. When I start to transform, do the same. Focus on the good and light and all that, though, and you should be able to do so without going dark."

"Show us where you're going in, and we'll find a good vantage point to be on standby," Elisa said. "Anything goes south, we'll come in—how did you put it?—weapons blazing."

Sharon nodded, gesturing to the theater house. "We have an entrance through there. If you're waiting at the edge of those trees," she indicated an area by a statue of a woman holding books to her chest, "you should be in a good position."

The ladies took their positions while Sharon and I entered the theater. Two students were on the stage in the middle of a scene from a play called Cabin 12. The rest of the class was too enraptured to even look our way. I could tell why, as the younger guy had started in about some football game and was kicking ass, getting all emotional about it. By my guess, the brother had been injured or killed.

Sharon pulled me by the sleeve, reminding me that we weren't there for the show. She led me around back, down to the side of the stage where the actors usually entered, and only then did the teacher see us. I noticed her stand to come after us, but then she seemed to have second thoughts, and sat down again.

Turning back to Sharon, I saw her giving a wave. She explained, "A guardian, but she knows me."

"And me?"

"She doesn't know you."

We continued to an area that looked like it was set up for props, and she pulled a lever. I had to laugh, as it totally had a whole set-piece feel to it. As we entered, I was taken back to my one semester as a stagehand in high school. Of course it had been a way to try to meet a girl, and when that hadn't panned out, I quit.

Stairs circled down into the ground in a way that brought me back to *DuckTales* memories, but before the end she put a hand on my chest and said, "Here."

"Transformation time?"

She nodded, hand still on my chest. "Are you ready?"

"I didn't know I had a choice."

"Good." With a grin, she closed her eyes, darkness coming over her.

"I thought—"

"That we could do it without the darkness?" she asked, voice hushed and pained, then she shook her head. "The key is to allow in just enough. Like when you know getting angry will help in a situation, but not letting it get the best of you."

I closed my eyes, focusing, but nothing happened.

Her eyes had a shadow to them, her hands trembling as she took mine, and she said, "The anger. Allow it in."

Our eyes met and I focused there, trying to think of nothing but transforming. But that was wrong. She said to let the anger in. I didn't know what to be angry about… at first. Then it started sweeping over me, how pissed I was at the thought that I'd come into this role without warning, that my ability to interact with my family was going to be incredibly limited going forward. Fuck that!

My chest convulsed as if I was gagging, my shoulders expanding and my hands clenching into fists.

Only, it was coming on too fast. I was seeing all of the fuckers who'd tried to kill us, all of the Shades and their bullshit, imagining killing them all and loving it. Pucky had stabbed that magic blade into my chest without warning, and... and... who the hell was I kidding, my life was awesome—at least, that's what I reminded myself of to pull myself together. And it was, truly. My mind went to the way Pucky laughed, the adoring smile of Elisa and the sensation of painting each other, and even Red with her silly Goth ways that all seemed a bit of a show now that I knew her.

The feeling of Sharon's hands in mine, as strong and clawed as they were, helped pull me back. I opened my eyes to see the werewolf version of her staring at me, and me as a werewolf in the reflection of her eyes. We'd done it, and neither of us was tearing into the other, so that was a good sign.

Without a word, she motioned me to follow her. Our hands fell apart, unfortunately, and then we were pushing through a rounded oak door into a den. A curved ceiling of dirt was overhead, several tunnels branching out from this wide room. There were a few thick blankets on one side of the room with men and women lounging on them, and it reminded me of the pictures of opium dens I'd seen.

As we drew closer, it became clear they weren't ordinary men and women, but trolls. They looked at us, apparently not finding any need to challenge two werewolves, before returning to their lazy afternoon. That worked well for us, and soon we were going down one of the hallways.

Here we passed a tall monster made of stone, its eyes glowing green and moving as it tracked me going past it. It grunted as it started to stand, grinding stones raising a commotion.

"Back off," Sharon said to it, standing in its way.

At first I thought she was talking to the golem, but then noticed her paw behind her, motioning me away. Maybe if it couldn't see me, we wouldn't have a problem? I did as she said, slipping into the curve of the passage behind, and coming to a small nook where a homeless-looking woman was riding a man, oversized breasts flapping about and fangs bared. I couldn't help but notice, as I drew closer, that the clothes on her back weren't clothes at all, but black feathers on folded wings.

They both turned to glare at me, so I looked away but kept moving past them.

"Night Raven," Sharon said as she caught up. "Found myself one, too."

Her hand found mine again, and now the woman —Night Raven, was grinning.

"Join us, then," Night Raven said. "No need for being shy."

"I'm eager to have him meet the witches," Sharon

countered, trying to squeeze between the two copu-
lating bodies and me.

"Nonsense," Night Raven said, wings spreading and
blocking our path while she continued to ride the guy.
"Come now, let's see what a werewolf cock looks like."

I gulped, not expecting this to be part of the
mission. Sharon growled, barely audible, and turned,
giving me an apologetic look. The expression on my
face was probably one of confusion, but I gave her a
slight nod. Damn, if this was what we needed to get
out of there, I wasn't going to argue.

"Careful you don't abandon yours, there," Sharon
said to her, stepping around and pulling at my
already stretched-out clothes. As I felt myself come
free, a gasp came from both ladies and a laugh from
the man, so I looked down and nearly jumped. Holy
fuck, did turning werewolf change things in more
ways than I'd known about.

The cock hanging out was mine, but about three
times larger than normal—and unfortunately hairy,
like one would expect from a werewolf. Sharon gave
me a look that had much more lust to it than before.
She took hold of me, showing it to the woman and
saying, "Now you understand why I'm really anxious
to get him to myself."

"No fucking way could I handle that thing,"

Night Raven said with a laugh, reaching down to pull the man's cock out of her. "I'll stick to tiny here," she laughed, gave it a short stroke, and then slid it back into her.

I expected him to be annoyed, but he shrugged and said, "Compared to that thing, even Conan would be small."

The compliments were great and all, but I hadn't yet decided if the fact that this wasn't my normal size was good or not. For one, if Sharon ever saw the real thing, she was bound to be disappointed. For now, she still had her hand on it and I was in bliss, a bit too distracted to really think of anything else or even focus on what we were doing there.

Good thing she put my cock away and said farewell, leading me on.

"Sorry," she whispered when we were down the hall and out of earshot from them. "I had to keep up appearances."

I chuckled. "Showing off the goods to strangers, but you touching me? Not something you'll ever have to apologize for."

Her eyes took me in, glanced down at my crotch again, and then she quickly turned around and kept walking.

"The main room is after this door," she explained. "So stay quiet, let me do the talking."

I agreed, naturally, and we entered to find a room that resembled an old tavern but without the bar. There were tables, several witches in a corner plotting with a map, and a swirling darkness on the ceiling in the center—an area I made sure to avoid. Taking a seat in the corner, Sharon hit the table twice and two drinks appeared.

"Don't actually drink it," she whispered in my ear, "but look like you are."

She made her way to the map, while I used my enhanced wolf hearing to see what I could pick up. It was immediately useful, aside from one witch describing the contents of some man's bowels after she'd gutted him. Others were discussing a 'she' forming an army, and I took that to mean Morganna, though I suppose it could've been referring to any number of evil villains. Some were preparing to join up with her, others wanted no part of it.

This was the most interesting part to me, because I'd been assuming it was a straight divide with all Legends united on one side, and all the Myths on the other. Listening to them argue about it, though, I soon came to understand that this wasn't the case at all. Some of them, and others out there, knew Morganna had served the agents as Riak, and therefore wanted nothing to do with her. She was tainted,

in their words. Others thought she might be planning something big, but couldn't be sure if it would
help them or hurt them. Some were all about joining
her just to be on the side with the power. Others
wanted to fight her, while still going up against
Myths and humanity.

My mind started lumping them into groups—the
truly evil, the chaotic evil, and the neutral chaotic.
How else could all of this make sense?

"As long as someone kills that damn Protector
and his friends, I'm happy," a green witch said,
passing my table and helping a very drunk-looking
flying monkey to walk. She moved her hand in a
circle and a portal appeared below the black swirling
area. They walked through the portal and were gone.

I tried not to show any sign of feeling that was
unusual or out of place, and was relieved to see
Sharon moving back my way. Her eyes turned dark
as she walked too close to the swirling black, but for
a brief flicker I saw the white of a swan over her
heart, and knew an internal battle was being won by
our side.

She reached me and her eyes were normal again.
"A powerful witch has him. Supposedly keeping
guard while the others debate how best to lure
you here."

"Funny," I said, glancing around and very glad

none of them had made the connection yet. If Pan had lived longer, or the others from the airport fight had managed to spread the news of my being able to go wolf, this group would've been on more of a lookout.

"You know where?" I asked.

She grinned, a horrible look on a werewolf, and then went first, me following a few seconds later. We passed several more doors and I had to wonder how many of these Legend hideouts there were, and how many Legends, for that matter. Sharon had explained to the group that many of them used portals to move around and tended to congregate where Myths were, so just because there were a lot here at the moment didn't mean it was always that way.

We stopped at the door Sharon indicated, pausing to prepare ourselves for a fight.

Yelping sounded from within, and my mind immediately went to images of Chris being tortured. No way was that going to happen on my watch. I charged the door, using my wolf strength to knock it down, and came in ready for a fight.

What I found was a reason to taste a bit of bile in my throat, but not in the horrible, friend being skinned alive way. No, more in the way that I'd never wanted to see my friend's hairy chode, but there it was, dangling balls and all, as he bent over, a witch standing behind him fingering his ass.

"Dude," I said, transforming back to myself.

Chris was bent over on his knees and forearms, but turned enough to look back at us and grimace before yelping once more. It was only then that I saw the witch was giving him a reach around, too.

"Can you give me like... thirty seconds?" Chris said.

The witch looked at us, down at Chris, then back to us, frozen, unsure what to do.

"No, we can't," Sharon said, brushing past me and grimacing at the sight. "And you, Hekate—right? What the fuck?"

"You've returned..." the witch Hekate still hadn't removed her hands, and Chris sighed in annoyance. "We thought we'd lost you."

"I was tracking this one down," Sharon said, motioning to me. "Now I'm back and find you're... doing whatever you're doing to this prisoner?"

"Hekate," I said, thoughtfully. "Where do I know that name?"

The witch beamed, tilting her wide-brimmed witch hat, finger still in his ass as she said, "Pleasure."

"Made famous by Shakespeare, like Puck-er-Pucky," Sharon said, and that triggered it.

"And Greek mythology," I said, excited. "Weren't you the goddess of ghosts and necromancy?"

"Among other things," Hekate said, grinning, finally pulling her hand away from Chris—much to his annoyance—to offer for me to shake. It was in this moment that I finally got a good glimpse of her as the light reflected to show her face. Dark, black eyes, skin a marble white with an almost unnatural smoothness. She wore a tight black and red dress, and a wide-brimmed, pointy hat. She was gorgeous and I felt this was a step up for Chris, ignoring the evil witch part. My gaze returned to her hand and I couldn't help but remember where her hands had just been.

"No offense, but I'll wait until you wash."

She shrugged, and wiped both hands together with a blue flash of magic, winked, and said, "Clean as can be."

"Seriously, after the way I went down on you," Chris said, standing with his erection in full view, no shame, "I don't even get to finish?"

"What's going on here?" I asked.

"I convinced Hekate here to give up her evil ways," Chris said with a laugh. "Shit, man, this role playing is intense! I mean, after they 'abducted' me, we came back here and she was my guard and well, one thing led to another."

Sharon eyed Hekate. "This is for real?"

"It might be," Hekate replied, taking a step back and raising her hands, eyeballing Sharon. "Are you going to try and stop us?"

"Actually, we came to save my friend," I replied, gesturing to Chris. "If he'd cover himself up, that is."

Hekate grinned at the sight of Chris nude, and Sharon turned toward me, chuckling. "Not how I expected this part of the mission to go."

"Clearly you don't know Chris," I replied, jokingly.

He just smiled, finally pulling up his underwear and pants, and said, "So what's the plan? How you busting me out of here?"

"I don't suppose you remembered to block the others out, did you?" Hekate asked, suddenly going even more pale.

"I'm not a witch," Sharon replied. "Don't have blocking spells."

"Well then." Hekate turned to the door and moved her hands, throwing up an invisible barrier just as a fireball hit it. "Time to vacate the premises."

"Can't you just make a portal?" I asked.

"Not while my magic's focused on them," Hekate replied.

"We make a run for it," Sharon suggested. "Jack, sound the alarm."

"Hit 'em on both sides," I said, nodding and wondering if I was ready yet, if Excalibur would help me in the fight somehow. "I like that."

"Now." She moved for the doorway as Hekate lowered the barrier, and then we were plowing through, Sharon and I roaring and attacking the witches while Hekate sent blasts of fire their way.

Shades popped up around the witches in their defense, and I tore through them, happy to get the prana from taking them out. Any extra power I could get before taking on Arthur and Morganna was more than welcome, and I was glad to see that I leveled up to four, along with getting an Ichor point.

More shouting and crashing sounded ahead, and then we saw bursts of light and a chunk of stone golem go flying, and Red and other two were there, fighting their way toward us. More Legends flashed in through portals, attacking and spreading Shades, and one yelled about alerting Morganna.

Red made a move to attack Hekate, but Chris threw himself in the way. "She's with me!"

"A topic I'm sure they'd very much like to hear more about," I said, gesturing my teammates onward. "But we need to keep moving."

"We have to get out of here before they call her in!" Hekate said, throwing flames at a flying monkey. "When I say go, go!"

"Who the fuck is this?" Red asked, but I just shook my head.

"Our best bet," Sharon answered for me, and then the portal was open and they all piled in while I went for more Shades.

"Now!" Hekate said, but I saw that Red was cutting through Shades too, the only other one of us left.

I grabbed her around the waist, pulled, and leaped into the portal.

5

Bursts of black light shot out as the portal faded behind us, and then it was gone. We found ourselves at the outskirts of the community college, the roar of the freeway not far off below. At least the location they had chosen was at the bottom of a hill that was cut off from view by what looked like a groundskeeper's shed, so nobody had seen us magically appear. Though, I supposed that if they had, we would've somehow made it look like we'd been there the whole time or something.

Elisa stared after the portal for a moment before turning to Chris.

"Explain."

"Allow me," Hekate said, but then pursed her lips in thought. Finally, she turned back to him. "Actually, dear?"

"Dear?" I asked.

Chris beamed. "What can I say, we hit it off." He put an arm around her waist. "Isn't she so sexy?"

"Um, yes," Elisa replied. "But… you know she's a witch, right? The evil kind?"

Hekate humphed and Chris held up a hand. "She's told me about her past, about—what was it— turning a bunch of kids into nightingales?"

"No, that was my sister Erqleen," Hekate said. "And they were all put back to normal."

"You see?" Chris shrugged as if that had somehow answered the question. "She's turned over a new leaf."

"I'm at least willing to try," Hekate added.

My gaze went to Sharon, then the others followed suit.

"What?" she asked.

"I mean, did you know her?" I asked. "You might be able to speak for her character."

"Hold on," Red said, holding up both hands and shaking her head. "We let in one bad apple, she tells us another one is fine, and before you know it they'll be in a prime position to slit our throats while we're sleeping."

"Red," Pucky said, shaking her head. "Legends can change, just as Myths have."

"We literally *just* let Sharon join us."

"I get it." Sharon frowned, but then nodded. "Trusting a Legend is tough… and another coming over so soon because she enjoys playing with this guy's asshole isn't exactly promising."

"For the record, not the reason," Hekate interjected. "A fun bonus, but not the reason."

"And the reason would be?" Elisa asked.

Hekate grinned and pinched Chris's cheek. "Have you seen his dimples? Come on, who could say no to this face." When she saw frowns, she added, "Fine, it's more than that. At first I was all like 'don't talk or I'll set a fire spell on you and watch your skin boil off your bones,' but then he kept talking and saying the sweetest things. But more than that, he told me about his buddy, Jack—the one he'd betrayed—and how sorry he felt. Went on about their time together, about friendship and loyalty, and how he'd give anything to make up for his betrayal, and I started thinking that maybe he could make up for it, and maybe I could make amends for everything I've done wrong, too."

"But you're a witch," Red said.

"And you're a fucking saint?" she countered with a glare that quickly changed into a smile. "Sorry, I'm trying here, but—wait, so you're on their side?" She stared at Sharon. "They let the Big Bad Wolf onto the team, but aren't sure about me?!"

"I was influenced by the shadows," Sharon replied sheepishly, but then snarled. "What's your excuse?"

"Lust for power," Hekate said, then held up a hand and turned, starting a spell that looked like it was closing the portal.

"And now a lust for these nuts is setting her free," Chris said, earning eye rolls from everyone.

"Whatever we do here," Elisa said, already starting to walk, "we need to move."

"And we're taking her with?" Red asked, irate.

"Honestly, I don't give a fuck. What I care about right now is that more don't show up. What's worse, us with only her, or us stuck with her and an army of more like her?"

Red scrunched her nose but started walking with the rest of us.

"To be clear, there are none *like* me," Hekate noted.

"She's right," Chris said, chuckling and taking her by the hand as they walked. He glanced my way and then looked away as he mumbled, "By the way, sorry about… you know. And thanks for coming for me."

"Don't worry about it," I said, very confused about our current situation but glad to know he wasn't being tortured by the enemy. From what we'd seen when we barged in on him, that hadn't been a concern regardless, but it was good to know.

I jogged to catch up with Elisa as she finished signaling the car. "Is it possible she has my friend under a spell?"

"Possible, sure, but I'd have sensed it." She took a moment, then stepped closer, making sure the others were a few steps back as she lowered her voice. "Honestly, I like the idea of having her on board, though we'd have to test her loyalty, of course."

"Oh?"

"First of all, I can't imagine the powers this one has. But even on a simple level, having access to their portals! Can you imagine? It means we don't have to rely on international teams—as long as there's a portal network in place she can tap into, we can go across the globe in an instant."

That left me thinking about the possibilities, although I had no idea what they could really mean. On the one hand, her statement had even larger implications. I hadn't even considered that other culture's fairy tales would be alive as well. Of course, most of the ones I knew had originated elsewhere, so the thought was silly to begin with. Hans Christian Andersen was Danish, Jakob and Wilhelm

Grimm from Germany. Peter Pan originated from a Scottish playwright.

And all of this put a new question in my head. "Elisa… are these Myths and Legends created by the stories, or…?"

"Discovered," she said. "Probably a better way to say it—which is also why not all of our realities match the stories you've heard about us. Many of us have existed for a long time, though some less so, and you can imagine the stories that have gotten around. Some authors finally started writing them down, and maybe they stuck to the facts, or maybe not."

"Which is kind of why gods aren't anything more than fairy tales," Pucky said, joining in the conversation. "For our purposes."

The others were all standing there now, listening.

I frowned. "But modern stories?"

"Some are just stories," Elisa replied. "Others… are very much real."

"Like that Justin Sloan book, *Hounds of God*," Sharon said. "So many werewolf characters are bullshit, but from that one? A lot of it was true—Kat is a badass, and a good friend. My only werewolf friend, actually, and helped me through a time in my life."

"Shit, I think I read that one," I said, trying to recall something about a woman and her journey to lead an army of werewolves against vampires and witches and whatnot. "She's still alive and fighting?"

Sharon frowned, glancing away. "It's complicated."

Red gave me a nod, but her look told me it was a topic for another conversation.

"Please tell me some of the P.T. Hylton books are real, or—"

Just then the car pulled up, and Pucky put a hand on my back. "We'll have time for all that," she said, and I sensed there was something weird about this topic—maybe they found something about how we viewed fairy tales offensive? The government *was* trying to hunt them down and kill them, after all.

I entered the car and let the topic rest, enjoying the fact that Chris went right into his normal way of taking over a conversation. He was Mr. Chatterbox, and totally into all of this even though he'd always treated my obsession with it before with a bit of contempt. Of course, that was before either of us had known there was truth to it.

It was a great opportunity to apply my recent promotion, so I brought up the screen. First I put the Prana toward speed and agility. Ichor was always more complicated, but one skill looked especially exciting, and led to even better ones—it seemed to be one that would absorb attacks and be able to channel the energy. Even better, it led down a path that allowed Tempest-focused group attacks. Looked like I had a new strategy, so I took the current upgrade and tuned back into the conversation.

"You two," Chris said, looking from Red to Sharon, "this is for real? The Big Bad Wolf and Little Red Riding Hood are now on a team?"

The witch looked curious as well, and even the rest froze waiting to hear the response.

"I'm not so 'bad' anymore," Sharon said, glancing hesitantly at Red.

"And I'm not so 'little,'" Red replied. "Big girls can make up their own minds on matters, and not be stuck to fairy tale bullshit."

"So you're okay with her being on the team?" Elisa asked.

"I haven't made up my mind yet."

Sharon chuckled nervously, but then added. "I'm just trying to make things right. Do good, you know? Because I've done enough bad that needs to be countered."

"And you weren't in complete control," Pucky reminded her.

Chris leaned over to Sharon. "Is it like being high? It is, right? I mean, there's got to be a reason it's so tempting once you've tasted it—the darkness."

"Your tone makes me worry about you," Sharon replied.

I jumped in, now that I'd had a bit of the taste myself. "It's nothing like that. Imagine more like you're having a dream and you're the bad guy, but you can't stop yourself. You're trying to wake up, escape the dream... but nothing works."

"Damn," he glanced over at Hekate. "And you're... in this dream now, or awake?"

She smiled sleepily, rolling her head as one does when drunk and trying to decide how drunk they really are. "Hmm, I'd say waking up."

"We'll keep an eye on you, and be sure to shake you good if you drift off again."

"Let's hope it doesn't come to that," Elisa said, glancing out the window. "But if it does, my brothers can help." At Chris's look of confusion, she explained, "they show up in the form of swans and bursts of light that help to fight the darkness. It's this whole thing."

"Right..." Chris pursed his lips, looking around at each of the ladies. "So you have to tell me —why him?"

"Forget you," I said, playfully hitting his leg.

"I'm serious. You're a great friend, really, I mean it. But a Protector? This—I mean, what are you? Best way I can see it, what with the humans after them and all, the Myths are like the Children of the Forrest and you're the new Night King. Not exactly, but—"

"Dude, fuck that," I replied. "You see me raising armies of the dead and marching off to kill humanity?"

"Not a perfect analogy, I concede." He grinned, clearly enjoying getting a rise out of me.

"It's different on many levels," Red said, then put her hand on my knee. "And to answer your question, it was partly because Excalibur had selected him, in a sense. And partly because the enemy knew it was him too—they have their own methods and... actually, Sharon?"

She blinked, confused, then frowned. "Oh, how did I know to go after him? A scent."

"I showered that morning," I protested.

"More like an internal scent," Sharon replied. "It was strong—maybe because of your connection with the Excalibur essence? I can't explain it, and honestly a lot of those memories are foggy."

Chris laughed, shaking his head. "Well, good thing our boy wasn't sick that day or you all would be out of a Protector."

"Maybe," Pucky replied. "Thing is, it's not like only one person fits—but the universe does have a way of putting all the right pieces in place. If he hadn't been there, maybe it wouldn't have been meant to be, and then maybe someone else would've been chosen. A woman, most likely."

"So you all didn't choose him, exactly," he said, grinning my way. "You're just stuck with him."

I was searching my mind for a comeback when Pucky came to my rescue.

"No, but we were the ones who choose to sleep with him."

Chris almost choked on his words when he said, "What?"

"Yeah, we don't usually fool around with the Protector, but…" Pucky blew a kiss my way.

When Chris's eyes settled on me, they were wide. "You're… I mean… with all of them?"

Not wanting to be the type to kiss and tell, I looked at Elisa as she nodded. "He's good, too."

Red lifted a finger. "Technically, I've not gone all the way yet, but look forward to it when it's time. We're fooling around."

Chris was staring in disbelief when his eyes moved over to Sharon. "You too?"

Sharon frowned, looked at me, and said, "I've only just joined the team, I'm not sure how that part works."

"We'll figure it out," Elisa said, earning a confused look from Red. I had to move in my seat to try and hide the growing boner that imagining fooling around with each of those ladies right then and there was causing.

Hekate noticed and grinned, putting an arm around Chris. "Don't be jealous. You'll have plenty of opportunities to play catch up."

Chris chuckled, taking his hand in hers. "It's not that, exactly. Okay, maybe a bit. But, more that…" He shifted to look at me. "You've never been much of a ladies' man."

"I was never the Protector either," I said. "And until very recently, fairy tales and whatnot didn't exist. So… anything goes, I guess."

He laughed. "Anything goes. Good for you, man."

When he put out his fist for a fist bump, I wasn't sure it was exactly acceptable, but Pucky took my wrist, helped me make a fist, and did it for me.

"Gotta accept praise when you get it," she said. "And hell, it's some accomplishment getting with us."

"Damn straight," Elisa said with a hearty laugh.

My libido was taking over, filling my mind with images of me and them rolling around in the car, flesh on flesh and moans of bliss escaping to cars nearby like exaggerated bass. If I didn't change the subject soon, I was likely to explode in my pants.

"What happens now?" I asked.

Elisa turned my way. "Meaning?"

"Well, Chris knows about you. About a lot of all this. So… do you do one of the *Men in Black* things and take away the memory?"

"Fuck you," Chris said.

"I'm just asking."

Elisa chuckled, considering Chris. "We could, though it's not exactly like that. I don't think we will though."

"No?" Chris perked up.

"You're a friend of the Protector's, and have been through a lot," Elisa said. "Even brought us a new recruit, in a sense." She glanced over at the witch, who put on her best smile, clearly trying. "What would it hurt to let you in on it? Knowing won't protect you, but—"

"Like Willow on *Buffy*," Chris said, full of excitement.

I laughed, though the others didn't get it. "Seriously, none of you watched *Buffy the Vampire Slayer*?"

"We're a bit busy saving the world most times," Red replied. "Shows and whatnot take a back seat to that more often than not."

"Point being," Chris said, holding out his fist to me again. "I accept."

I chuckled and gave him a fist bump without help this time, then leaned back and watched as we made our return. Red insisted Hekate wear a blindfold, though I very much wondered if it mattered, since the woman was a witch and all.

When we were close, we saw it was too late, anyway. Smoke rose in the distance. I knew it was the safe house before we got close enough to see it.

6

We had the car let us out two blocks away and worked through the less-crowded streets, noting the people gathered and pointing. There was a firetruck with lights flashing out front of the house when we arrived.

"Mowgli, we're outside," Red said into her comms.

"Good timing," he replied.

"You could've used the comms at any time," she shot back, not hiding the annoyance in her voice.

"True," he replied, appearing at the side of the supposed safe house and coming to meet us. "But that's exactly what they would've wanted, I imagine."

We all shared a look of confusion. Elisa was the one to say, "Explain."

"Consider the fact that Arthur can track Excalibur." He let that linger. "Now if that's the case, why did they choose to attack here during the small window of time that you were gone?"

I ran a hand through my hair, trying to figure out this riddle. "He can't?"

"No, we're sure of that ability," Elisa said.

"Although," Mowgli said, thoughtfully, "it's possible that when Jack became a Tempest the sword formed a bond with him, in a sense, and therefore Arthur's bond was broken. But I don't think so."

"Right," Red agreed. "This is Arthur and Excalibur we're talking about here."

"So why then?" I asked.

Mowgli shook his head. "I'm still trying to figure that one out. Maybe they were after something other than the sword or you? Maybe they figured we'd move the sword to lead them off your trail, so attacked hoping they'd find you? It's a mystery we'll find the answer to, but for now I can't shed light on."

"It's a good thing he *was* gone," a woman's voice said, appearing out of nowhere to Mowgli's left a second later. She had a shimmering blue to her, with pointed ears and eyes of green. I imagined she was some sort of spirit or fairy. She looked me up and down, smirked, and said, "He's not strong enough yet. Would've been killed for sure."

"Hey," I protested, but Mowgli scrunched his nose, showing the spirit wasn't the only one who thought so.

"We're relocating," Mowgli said, gesturing over to several cars that were arriving behind us. "Under the cover of magic," he added when I glanced at the sky. "She might be able to track us with the sword anyway, but we're not sure what that situation is anymore, so we'll take our chances."

"And then?" Pucky asked.

He grinned. "Three Ninja's Strike Back."

"You do watch movies!" I exclaimed, excited. "I mean, from a long-ass time ago, but hey, not bad. Kinda."

"I'm not following," Chris admitted, which didn't surprise me. His knowledge of film extended to anything with celebrity titty shots, his favorite being some corny one from the nineties with Kevin Bacon —I liked to point out that he probably liked it for the Kevin Bacon full-frontal, but he only laughed it off and never denied it, so I left the topic alone.

After a second of Mowgli standing proud and me grinning, Pucky said, "So… that means we are the ninjas in this movie?"

"Yes, and we're going to find a way to track her down," Mowgli answered, "find a way to end this." He led us toward a car, only then glancing at the witch and saying, "I imagine there's a good reason a witch is coming with us?"

"We'll tell you in the car," Elisa replied.

The ride was uneventful. We filled him in, and he expressed his worry over the recent attack, and how he felt it was like going back a step in the war. At the moment, Morganna had a major advantage over us, so outside-the-box thinking would be needed to regain our advantage.

Before long we were pulling up at our new location. I was excited to see that it wasn't just a random house or movie-lot stage this time, but a badass oceanfront property.

"How the hell do you all afford this?" I asked, stepping out of the car, Chris whistling at my side.

"Old money," Mowgli said, nodding at Elisa. "Some of the Originals, especially, have been around for so long, investing in the right endeavors along the way... you'd blow your mind trying to understand how rich they are."

Elisa frowned his way, apparently having heard. "My affairs are my own business, Mowgli." She gave me a grin. "But yeah, I'm, how do you youngsters say it? 'Rich as fuck.'"

I laughed, though it turned into a nervous chuckle. The thought of her being rich didn't intimidate me, but I had to wonder how old she really was.

My humor turned to true awe when we entered to find that the interior was essentially a more Atlantis-themed version of the other fancy house of hers we'd been in. It didn't have the massive nude painting of her, unfortunately—I could walk up and down hallways like that all day!—but was complete with a swan-shaped chandelier, a courtyard with a fountain of seven swans surrounding Elisa in the center in such a way that their wings covered her where clothes would've done if the statue had any. At times I had to wonder if she was really this narcissistic to have so much about her or related to her magic, but I knew her too well for that.

Heading back to the rooms while Mowgli and others set up new defenses and called in reinforcements, we found a snack room and gathered around, hydrating and filling up on protein shakes that Pucky put together. I snagged a Gala apple and sat back, glad to be in one place again, even if it was only going to be for a bit before we figured out our plan of attack against Morganna and Arthur.

"I'm almost sorry you got wrapped up in it all," Hekate said, reaching under the table in a way that was way too obvious, made more so when Chris's eyes went wide. "Of course, if you hadn't, we never would've met."

"I'll take it," Chris said with a silly grin, but then

worry creased his face. "Though… it hasn't been all rainbows and sunshine."

"You mean rimjobs and—" I started, but Elisa gave me a look that shut me up real fast. Who was I to talk?

"You're lucky they didn't hurt your family," Elisa said to Chris. "Since you're not a Myth or Protector, there isn't much our magic can do."

"Great, I'll do that," Chris said. "Become a Myth."

I laughed, but noticed that Elisa wasn't laughing.

She looked at the witch by Chris's side. "He doesn't have a clue what he's asking, does he?"

"No," the witch said, already looking uneasily at Chris. "No idea what it would mean for him, or me."

"What does she mean?" I asked. "Can someone, a normie, become a Myth?"

"It's happened, but… he has to take it from someone, and have a pure heart in the process. If he were to take it from one of us, for instance, he would automatically be an evil Legend, because there's no way he could do it without doing so for the wrong reasons."

"So I have to basically kill a Legend?" Chris asked, eyes going wide.

"Pretty much. But even then you'd need the pure heart thing."

"I'm not convinced you have that part covered," I cut in, joking around but partially serious.

"Dude, who stepped in to get your back when that prick was picking on you in the dorms? Who covered half your rent when you were a little low?"

"Not sure that stuff covers all the requirements." I turned to Elisa, wondering what the standards were.

"Just tell me what I need to do, and I'll do it," Chris said. "Come on, Jack. Get my back. Tell her you know I have a pure heart and all that." I hesitated, but he leaned in close. "Man, this is about my family. My sister, Jen. And everyone else the Legends might hurt. I want to fight these punks, to show them they can't mess with fucking 'normies' anymore."

"Please," I said to Elisa.

That did it. She nodded, then turned to the witch. "Hekate, was it?"

Hekate nodded.

"And… can you go back with a disguise, without the other Legends knowing it's you?"

"I'm not sure," Hekate admitted. "Though, with my powers…"

"And our help," Elisa cut in, nodding to herself.

"What's happening, exactly?" Chris asked.

"You'll go undercover with her," Elisa said. "The two of you will have a very important mission, one that will ensure you get your Myth status... or fall to the darkness trying. Let's plan on the former, shall we?"

Hekate appeared deeply troubled by this, but Chris was nodding enthusiastically, more than ready for this moment.

7

T he conversation carried on for a while, finally wrapping us back to the topic of Morganna.

"She might attack again, or she might not," Elisa said. "They attacked at a time when they knew Jack wasn't here …I just don't understand what she's up to. I have no idea what she'll do next."

"Her next strike could be anywhere," Red said, nodding in agreement. "We need to find her before that happens."

"Seeing as she's your sister," Mowgli said, turning to Pucky. "Any thoughts here? Where do we start?"

"Bullshit," Pucky shot back. "You know that the moment she merged with Morganna, her mind could be going that direction as much as my sister's. Even if that weren't the case, I've been out of touch with my sister ever since she started helping the agents."

He frowned. "Your best guess?"

"With the agents."

Mowgli sighed, eyeing me for a moment, then Chris. He sighed again then, turning to the table and taking a seat. "Let's think here, people. If she's with the agents, an attack on them might be the right move, but that's huge. We have to weigh each possibility."

"Maybe we're looking at the wrong Legend?" Pucky said. "Arthur, the Lady of the Lake…?"

I wanted to hear this, but honestly my bladder was about to explode, so I excused myself and went for the restroom. The downstairs one was occupied, so I made my way upstairs and took care of business.

When I came out, Red was there and gave me a sigh and shrug before going in. I walked over to the railing that overlooked the floor below, watching as the others continued to discuss their options and what going for the Lady in the Lake would do. They seemed to move on to other ideas, and a moment later Red joined me.

She motioned me to follow and we went to one of the outer patios instead, looking out over the ocean. The beach shimmered in the light, a low roar of waves carrying up and making me wonder if sleep would be a good idea—it felt so peaceful. The sun warmed my face, and I closed my eyes, simply enjoying it for a moment.

"It's too bad we can't stay here a while and take a vacation," Red said, and I opened my eyes to see she was watching me, smiling. It was the first time I'd found myself alone with her in a while, and for some reason it felt awkward. She was frowning, staring at the wall while her tongue played with her lip piercing.

"Shouldn't we be in there?"

She shook her head. "That won't lead anywhere. It's not so simple, that's why I wanted to come out here. Let the fresh air open up my mind, help me think outside the box."

I stood next to her in silence for a moment, thinking about what she'd said. But as the wind blew through my hair, my mind wandered to her and the way our relationship worked. It was strange that we hadn't spent more time one on one, and that even when with the others, there was something different about her.

Finally it hit me why, and I turned to her, wondering how to ask this. "Red…?"

"Yeah?"

"You have something against me?"

She turned, surprised. "What?"

"I mean…" I shifted uncomfortably, cracking my neck. "Does something feel off here to you?"

"No." Her frown deepened, and she looked genuinely offended.

"That's not how I meant it."

"How did you mean it then, Jack? Because it sounds like you're saying you don't feel a connection, or that—"

I stepped in, reaching first to see if she'd stop me, and then took her face in my hands and kissed her. She didn't resist, but stared at me with wide eyes even as her tongue met mine. When I pulled back, she frowned, smiled, then frowned again.

"And what was that?" she asked.

"See, this is where I'm confused. There was passion, yes? A spark?"

She tried not to smile, but nodded.

"Okay, so then here's the thing—before, don't tell her I said anything…"

"Spit it out, Jack."

"Right." I glanced around, ensuring Pucky wasn't there. "Well, I kinda heard you were more… open to sex than you've put on. So…?"

"That bitch," Red said, flushing instantly and turning back the way we'd come.

"No, it's not—"

"She told you I was slutty, didn't she? Loose? Something like that?"

I racked my brain to come up with a lie, a way out of this, but nothing worked. "'Biggest slut I know,' were her exact words, I believe."

"That bitch…"

"The point being," I said, trying to bring the conversation back to where it was meant to be, "that doesn't exactly add up with… us."

Her angry glare turned my way, and she held it there a moment before saying, "Are you asking why I haven't put out yet? Shit, man. How long have we known each other?"

"No, I don't mean it like that. Of course, that makes sense. I'm only trying to understand—"

"Well stop, okay." Red said, turning and glaring. "You want to know what… if I've slept with a lot of men? Here it is—of course! I'm hot, I'm a Myth, and I need to release steam sometimes after running from the fucking government agents or fighting Legends. So what's the point?"

"That's not what I wanted to know," I countered, pulling my wrist away and glaring right back at her. "On the list of things I'd want to hear, that's at the bottom. What I'd like to know is why not me? If all that's true and you are so open with it all, well… it just doesn't make sense."

"Right." She turned, took off her hood, and leaned over the railing, looking down at a cat running by. "The others fuck you because they care. I don't fuck you because I care."

"Huh?"

She reached a hand out to me, not even looking. When I took it, and stood next to her, she continued. "Those other guys were what I said—blowing off steam. I don't want you to be just another one of them, you know? You... there's a connection with you. "

"And the others?"

"What would it matter?" She scoffed. "You have other women."

"Maybe it wouldn't?" I said, though the words caught in my mouth. "Still... I'd like to know."

She shook her head. "For one, I'm with you fighting jackasses all the damn time, how could I?"

"And for two?"

She smiled at me, but quickly looked away again, squeezing my hand. "I don't want anyone else."

It felt like a good moment to kiss her, and I was turning to make my move, when she suddenly straightened, her eyes following the cat.

"I've got it," she exclaimed.

"What?"

"Our answer. Sekhmet." She was already running

back through the doors before I had the chance to ask what the hell she'd just said to me. I followed, and raced into the main room where she came to a stop, practically panting with excitement. Everyone paused, turning to her as they sensed something was up.

"If we're going to have any hope of finding Arthur," Red said, grinning, "we'll need some pussies."

"What?" I said from behind, caught off guard by that.

"Of course!" Mowgli laughed, nodding, though some of the others still looked confused. "That's just her lewd way of saying we need to find Sekhmet."

"Again... what?" Others seemed to understand Red's statement, but the name Sekhmet was lost on me.

"There's a whole hell of a lot that goes into answering that question," Mowgli said, leaning forward. "The simple answer is that she was an Egyptian Legend, a goddess, according to them."

"Like how Thor is a god, but... not really?"

"It's all relative," Mowgli said. "I mean, is a certain level of power and magic what makes someone a god? Per their religion, yes, she was a goddess, but she was no more from some heavenly realm than you or I."

"Explain the pussy comment," Pucky said, still grinning at Red for that one.

"Cats," Red said. "Sekhmet wasn't just the daughter of Ra—another Legend that has since been killed off, by the way—she was, or is, a tracker. There's a reason cats were said to serve as guardians of the underworld in Ancient Egypt, and that was because of their ability to track those Myths and Legends who were reborn, such as Arthur, or absorbed back like Riak did with Morganna."

"And Sekhmet can do this?"

"Her sister, Bastet, can," Elisa said, nodding, getting into this. "And rumor has it Bastet was cursed, unable to ever leave the form of a cat—and that Sekhmet now watches over her."

"So we have to find Sekhmet, and her sister the cat," Pucky said, nodding. Even Mowgli seemed to buy this.

"Only one problem," he said.

"I know," Red cut him off. "Finding her. But she's missing two items, both of which she'd do anything to have back. I happen to know where to find one of them."

The others leaned in, eagerly. It looked like we had our mission.

8

"The Sekhem Scepter of Power," Red said, as we all joined together in the enclosed courtyard, ready for Hekate to prepare the portal. "It had been used in burial rituals, waved over powerful dead to put a spell on them and keep them that way."

"That way meaning… dead?" I asked.

"Exactly." Turning to Hekate, she asked, "If we can get her scepter, you can make a portal to her?"

"All it takes is an item that was close to the subject," Hekate said. "And then yes."

"Then we're in business."

"And the other item?" I asked.

"I don't know where it is, but heard she had lost it, too. The sun disk, with the Uraeus rearing cobra."

"Last I heard," Elisa said, "it was taken by the new Wadjet, or Buto. The serpent goddess."

"Who was defeated in the Vietnam War," Mowgli said with a frown.

"What the fuck?" Chris mumbled next to me, and I just held up a hand, telling him it was better not to ask—that rabbit hole could be left for a long car ride or trek across the desert.

"The focus here is on the scepter, because I know where to get it," Red said. She then took her dagger and asked, "You can make a portal to the person who made this?"

Hekate frowned, but nodded.

"I'm not following," Elisa admitted.

"The man who made this blade happens to collect magical items," Red explained. "He had this dagger, until I nicked it. He wasn't exactly the giving type and I figured he owed me when…" She glanced at me, frowned, and said, "Let's just say he pissed me off."

"She means she went down on him and he passed out after without returning the favor," Pucky whispered into my ear. Chris overheard and chuckled, but Red kept on without paying us any attention.

"I'll have to watch my magical knives next time that happens," Chris whispered back, earning him a nudge from Hekate.

"That won't *ever* happen," she said, glaring. He kissed her on the lips.

"Can we focus?" Red said, and other Myths were looking our way, so I took a step sideways and joined in with the glaring at Chris thing, which he rolled his eyes at but at least he shut up.

"Do it," Elisa said to Hekate. "Please. And Red, how many do we need?"

"Our small team should do," Red said, nodding to me and Pucky, then glancing at Sharon with trepidation.

"Sharon proved quite useful at the college," I spoke up before I'd had time to think about it. But hey, she had and deserved her spot on the team.

"Agreed," Elisa said. "But we'll also need Hekate to open the portal from the other side."

"Leaving me, what… here?" Chris asked.

"You have no powers, and you're not a Protector," Mowgli said. "It would be unwise to send you into danger."

"But I can—"

"Mowgli's right," Elisa said sharply, shutting down any chance Chris had. I was guessing her authority stemmed from her being one of the originals. "But…"

Chris perked up. "I like buts."

Even Hekate rolled her eyes that time.

"But," Elisa continued, "I have a mission for you later, when we get back and with Hekate on board… well, let's just say it would be a great test for both of you."

"Test?" Hekate said scornfully.

"You *did* just join us based on lust for Chris. You have to admit it would be foolish to trust you right away."

"What did you have in mind?" Chris asked, before the witch could protest further.

Elisa shared an approving look with Mowgli, leading me to believe they'd already discussed the idea, then said, "You'd infiltrate the witches… and become one."

Hekate couldn't be silent for that. "You know what that means! You'd ask me to—"

"What, betray your sisters?" Pucky cut in.

"No, er… It's complicated."

"But if you're on our side," Elisa said, "then it isn't. He doesn't have to kill anyone, not if you can get the three leaves. Of course, there's so much more to it, isn't there?"

Hekate nodded, glaring at Elisa. "You all look at me like I'm some random witch. Well guess what? Not all Legends are there by choice—most of us witches got lumped in because we're not perfect. All of you are? I doubt it. Have I done horrible things?

Despicable? Certainly! But I'm here to turn over a new leaf, and no, not just because Chris here is hot and sexy and there's something about him being tied up that gets my steam going."

"Too much information," Pucky hissed.

"You want me to prove myself?" Hekate said, ignoring her. "Fuck it. Point me in the right direction."

"We'll talk specifics when it's time," Elisa said with a satisfied grin. There was something else to that smile, a victorious, almost gloating look I hadn't seen on her before. It didn't quite fit the often calm, take-charge type woman I'd started to know her to be.

It was hot.

"How long will it take you to make the portal?" Red asked.

Hekate held out her hands, accepting the dagger. She closed her eyes and a dull glow emitted from the blade. "It's been some time since it was in his hands. I'd say it'll take at least thirty minutes."

"Please begin."

"Everyone prepare defenses and set up comms in case they come again," Mowgli said, addressing the others. Then he turned to us and said, "We at least know what to expect this time, so should be ready, though I don't expect another attack like that again."

"We'll prepare," Elisa said. "I have some armor for the boys."

"Armor?" Chris said, excitedly.

"Boys?" I said, with less enthusiasm. Even if I was potentially centuries younger than her, it didn't sound right.

She smiled, running a hand along my chest and looking me in the eyes as she said, "Sorry. Men."

"Call me a baby, I don't care," Chris said. "Just point me to the armor."

Hekate gave us a sideways, jealous glance as we headed back with Elisa, but then returned her focus to the dark waves of energy starting to form in front of her.

In the lobby, Elisa waved over a short man who was dressed like one of the Munchkins and said, "Did you manage to grab it?"

He grinned and handed over a black gym bag before replying in a squeaky voice, "I had to run back in, but you made it sound important. What's in there, anyway?"

"Shirts," she said with a laugh.

He frowned, but his eyes went wide when she unzipped the bag and pulled out two shirts of nettles.

"These were originally made to break curses," she said, handing one to me and the other to Chris. "I had made them for Jack, but you might need it where you're going."

"Am I going to find out more about that?" he asked, accepting the shirt and then yelping, instantly dropping it. I wasn't sure what to do with the thing, as holding it was like holding a ball of needles, but made sure not to drop it or grip it too tightly.

Elisa, to her credit, simply laughed. "You'll have to get used to it, but the pain is fleeting. Come, remove your shirt."

He glanced back toward the door, uncertain. "Um…"

"Are you worried I'll try to seduce you, or put the shirt on you?"

"Both?"

"Only the latter," she assured him, though I had to admit that didn't sound great. "That is, unless you want to return to your family and put them at risk. When you're one of us, our magic keeps them from being found, but if you're not…"

He grumbled, removing his shirt and standing there, waiting. I wasn't sure what to expect, but jumped when she pulled the shirt over his head and lines of red followed. Grunts of pain came from within the shirt, and then his face was exposed and it was covered in blood—straight nasty, and she kept pulling the shirt!

"The fuck are you doing?" I asked, grabbing her arm and about to step in.

"Trust me," Elisa said with a reassuring stare.

I did, as crazy as that seemed at that moment, so I released her arm and stepped back, still in shock. Only, as I looked at Chris the shirt was morphing around him, not even needing his arms for the sleeves, and the wounds on his face had healed, the blood gone.

He stared at her in confusion, blinking.

"Is the pain gone?" she asked.

"Yes," he said, meekly.

"Magic. That's the price." She adjusted the shirt, and it took on the look of a tan, cloth shirt. "Only put it on in private, as you'll experience that same sensation each time. This will tells us once and for all if the witch has put a curse on you or any sort of spell to earn your affection."

"Her name is Hekate," he said, annoyed. "And of course she didn't."

"But now we'll know for sure," Elisa said. "And even if you already do, I have to be as positive as you are."

"A small price for me to pay for your peace of mind," he said, his sarcasm clearly missed by her, as evidenced by her smile.

"And why do I need one?" I asked.

"You don't, necessarily," she admitted. "But… it can fight off the werewolf. Sharon has agreed to take one as well, though… if she wants to transform now, she'll have to take it off—which could be awkward in the middle of a fight."

I tried to not imagine Sharon tearing off her shirt mid-fight, to keep my mind focused on anything other than the thought of her breasts jiggling as she prepared to kick ass. Trying was futile, and Elisa had to laugh.

"Be more obvious, next time," she said, earning a blush from me.

"Hey, your fault—not mine."

"Yes, well… She's in, you know."

I frowned, unsure where she was going with that and not wanting to be presumptuous. "In…?"

"The team. We'll talk with the others, but I'm sure they'll come around. Red is the most hesitant, but Sharon would like to be part of it, I can tell, and I want to make it happen for her.

Chris gave me a very impressed look, but then frowned again. "Wait, still… me. What's this got to do with where I'm going? Are you going to clue me in now?"

"Right." Elisa grinned, motioning to his shirt. "You're going to infiltrate the witches' coven. You wear this when you go there, even under your other clothes.

He frowned, totally confused, but nodded.

I had to admit—if I'd not recently found the most amazing life ever for myself, I might have been jealous. It sounded like he was basically about to live the much darker version of every 'boy goes to witch school' story ever told. A very dark version, where he had to scrape his face with thorns whenever he wanted to be sure to break a curse, it seemed.

"Why not always keep the shirt on?" I asked. "For him, I mean."

"All the sex, for one," she replied, as if that was obvious.

He stared, glanced down at the shirt, and seemed to like it that much more already.

"Sorry, the…?" I started.

"Yeah, of course. He's going to find his coven. Not all are like this, but yeah, you're going to have to get into some very sexual, very dark rituals that are going to push you to your very limits. You know, sexual limits. Oh, is that—sorry, I didn't even think about it. Will that be a problem, Chris?"

Chris shook his head vigorously.

"Good, it's settled."

"And my shirt?" I asked.

"You don't have to wear it now," Elisa said. "But

when the shadows are strong, the wolf coming out, or you anticipate going up directly against Shades? That'd be the time."

"Got it." I glanced down at in my hands, frowning. "And until then?"

She laughed. "The advantage of magical shirts. Just fold it up."

I scrunched my nose, knowing this was going to hurt, and fucking A it did. Each fold tore at my fingers and hands, but soon I had it in a smaller square than I would've thought possible, and it took on the look of a pocket square. I fit it into the back pocket of my jeans, and was ready to go. Just as the wounds had healed on Chris though, so too, did those on my hands.

"The price," I said, looking them over.

"A small blip on the larger pain scale of life," Elisa said with a grin, holding up her own hands to show the scars. "Not all magic prices are temporary."

We nodded, accepting that lesson, and after a moment Chris asked, "When do I, er, go off to this wizarding school?"

"Wizarding school?" Elisa said with a laugh, then thought about it. "Actually, in a way you will be a wizard, won't you? I mean, they'll think of you as a warlock, but since you'll really be on our team—and that better not change—you'll be a wizard. Interesting."

"And badass as fuck," Chris said, but cringed. "Ooh, sorry."

"The language?" Elisa laughed. "Dear, in my time I've heard much worse, trust me. Come, keep your gifts hidden—yes, even from Hekate, Chris. Until you have no doubts, don't trust anyone with absolute one hundred percent certainty… and maybe not even then."

"Understood."

"Now, Jack, we have business to attend to before we leave. Need to check our weapons and all that."

I started to protest that I knew for a fact Excalibur was fine and ready to go, until I noticed her wink and a quick glance at my crotch.

"And Chris?" I asked.

"I think he and Mowgli should talk before we head out. We'll meet back up when the portal's ready."

Chris gave me a nod and a knowing smile, then jogged off to find Mowgli.

"All that planning and myth lore talk," she said, stepping close to me and running her hand along my abs, around to my back. She reached down and grabbed my ass so that my hips were pressed against her. "It works up an appetite."

"We'll have to make sure you're fed properly," I said, feeling like such an idiot. This kind of sexy talk thing was not in my comfort zone in the slightest.

Her smile showed she didn't care, and with a deep breath she turned, grabbing me by the belt and leading me through the halls.

When we found Red and Pucky playing cards, she motioned for them to come along, and both followed, excitedly.

"Get Sharon," Elisa said, stopping at some double doors.

"Are you sure?" Pucky asked.

"I'm not—" Red started, but Elisa grabbed my crotch and kissed my neck before saying, "Don't be a dick, Red. Just bring her."

Elisa opened the doors and led me in, the other two still lingering behind.

"I don't want to make Red feel uncomfortable," I whispered.

"She'll be into it. Trust me."

"Yeah, but…" I really had nothing to add, and so far every time this woman said to trust her, it had worked out for the best.

A glance around and I saw that she'd led me to a room that was decorated in Elisa's familiar taste but with the added dash of a Moroccan theme. Silk sheets hung from the ceiling and surrounded beds full of cushions, but everything was white like the swans.

"This is necessary," Elisa said, "for all of us."

Red entered next, still looking hesitant, and then Pucky with Sharon. The latter froze, seeing what was happening, and bit her lip.

"Necessary?" Red asked, a glare directed toward Sharon.

"Could be the last time for a while," Elisa said. "Who knows what could happen."

She was the first to remove her clothes, stepping away to give me a show as she dropped them to the floor and turned to me, hands outstretched. I walked toward her, taking her hands and kissing them, moving along her left arm to her breasts. Sometimes perky works for my mood, and right then they were perfect. My hands moved to caress her, feel her nipples between my fingers as I stood to kiss her. Our tongues met as I felt another mouth kissing my neck and, judging by what felt like a horn on the back of my head, it was Pucky. Hands were working my clothes, and I glanced down to see my erect cock emerge for a second before Pucky had it in her mouth. Red stood by, not sure what to think, it seemed, as her eyes kept darting to me and then over to Sharon.

Lips nibbling at mine, Elisa saw this too, and

pulled back, kneeling to join Pucky as she pushed my mouth toward Red. The latter accepted, kissing me and letting her guard drop, so that by the time Pucky motioned to Sharon and had pulled her into the mix, it was too late for Red to argue.

When Red pulled away from me kissing her neck, I thought she was going to say something about Sharon—who was hesitantly running her arms along mine. I was surprised to see Red step up behind her, reach a hand down her pants, and start caressing Sharon's mound.

Sharon looked astonished too, but the others were smiling, licking my cock and balls, then my hips, and turning my cock for her to take.

"Get on your knees," Red said, more forcefully than I was used to from her. I did, while Pucky finished undressing and moved behind me with Elisa, both kissing my back and caressing me, watching to see what Red had planned. None of us were used to this side of her.

Red pulled at Sharon's pants and then panties, and I wasn't surprised in the least to see an ungroomed bush down there—though watching Red's fingers spread the lips apart and move into her was quite the sight. Red caressed her while Sharon's eyes moved across me, from eyes to cock and then she was taking the initiative, bending over and having me lie down, so that she was over me, and her hand took my cock. She stared at it, fingers caressing the sides of the shaft, and then—as Red fingered her from behind, Sharon leaned over and ran her tongue along my balls, hand starting to stroke me.

"Fucking A," Pucky said, rubbing her tits and then leaning over to let me kiss them, as I took my hands and started fingering her and Elisa.

Sharon was into it, but seemed uncomfortable, blushing as her eyes moved about, nervously. I took her face in my hand and pulled my hips back.

"You're not ready?" I asked.

She looked hesitant, then said, "I am."

"If she was, she wouldn't have hesitated," Elisa said, moving over to me and laying me back, straddling my hips and sliding my cock inside of her. "It's okay," she told Sharon, "watch, enjoy. Get comfortable. Next time, maybe you'll want to join in."

At that, Elisa started moving up and down on my cock, and I was lost in the bliss of it all. Sharon actually did look relieved to be watching, though Red looked almost embarrassed by the situation—maybe even mad?

My chest was clenched, anticipation rising when Elisa started moaning. She came first, though I knew

I was close, and Pucky hopped on next as if they were taking turns at the theme park that was me.

She started slowly, seeing that I was close to climax, while Red and Sharon watched, Sharon simply enjoying the show while Red was touching herself in a way that turned me on even more. There was no way I was going to last, so I pulled Pucky in for a passionate kiss and then whispered, "I'm going to cum," and she smiled, nibbled on my ear, and then rolled me over on top of her, so that when she grabbed my cock and squeezed, before she'd even gotten one good stroke in I was exploding all over her breasts and stomach. She laughed, Red moaned while massaging her clit furiously and finally reaching orgasm, too, and I lay back, closing my eyes.

"No rest for the wicked," Elisa said, grabbing a box of tissues and handing them to Pucky. "It's time."

I pouted, wanting to take time to ensure Pucky got hers, but she noticed my reaction and squeezed my arm as she cleaned herself and said, "Next time. Trust me, I'll survive."

As they dressed, I found a bathroom to wash up, and on the way out spotted Pucky and Sharon talking, then noticed Red walking off.

"Is she going to be okay?" I asked. Turning to Sharon, I added, "And... you?"

"This is all new to me," Sharon admitted. "But, as weird as it was, it was equally amazing." Her eyes went to the floor and she mumbled, "I'm looking forward to next time."

"Me too," I admitted, and smiled before excusing myself to check on Red. There was no time, however, as Red was with Hekate when I caught up, and that sort of conversation didn't feel right in front of a witch I'd just met—even if she had been getting nasty with my best friend when we'd first met. Raincheck, then.

The others caught up a few moments later, and we were ready to head off.

9

Going through the portal was much like it had been with the pizza place when saving Elisa. We stepped in and were through, finding ourselves in a penthouse suite that spoke of immense wealth. The walls were lined with masks from Africa, swords and suits of armor that looked like they ranged from medieval Europe to the Middle East, and paintings scattered throughout as well. My ladies were particularly interested in a set of glimmering gold jewelry, one of twisted metal that looked like a necklace, the other like a crown.

I'll admit, all of this stuff was nearly enough to make me forget about what I'd wanted to talk to Red about. To say I was overwhelmed was an understatement—it was like having only ever seen vanilla ice

cream your whole life and then one day walking into
Ben & Jerry's.

"You mentioned he was a collector," I said, "but
damn. This is like a museum."

"He's had a damn long time to collect it all," Red
said, hand on the blade in her belt. "After the forty
thieves' treasure, he just never stopped."

"Wait…" I turned to her, jaw dropping before I
managed to get out, "You're telling me this is all Ali
Baba's stuff?"

She nodded. "As long as Morgiana isn't around,
we should be safe. She's ruthless."

"Wait, Morganna?"

"Similar name, but no. No relation."

I nodded, glancing over at Pucky and Elisa, who
were already moving around cautiously, searching
for the scepter. Hekate stood at the ready, eyes alert.
I couldn't see Sharon since she was behind me, but I
could hear her quiet footsteps.

"You sensing something?" I asked.

The others looked over now too, and we waited.
Finally, Hekate nodded, pointing to the hallway
opposite my position.

"A ward," she said. "They'll be here soon."

"Search fast," Red said.

"It won't matter." Hekate moved to the hallway,
kneeled and started to draw a line in the wood with

one of her fingernails, an act that made me cringe. "I'll do what I can to set up counter-wards, to stall them."

"And who's them, exactly?" I asked, joining in the search.

"Morgiana married Ali Baba's son, a man who she trained in the ancient art of sword fighting known as the river dance—roughly translated." Red cursed, having found a box hidden below some of the shelves, but it only contained a series of goblets. "Both are now known in these parts as the type not to fuck with."

"And they're not on our side?"

"Neutral-good," she said. "Which is better than neutral-chaotic, as some of those back at the community college were, but they'd still rather fight us than let us walk away with the scepter."

"How do you know if you don't ask?"

"Shut up and help me find it." She stood, stepping back and analyzing the wall in front of her, which had shelves with vases, several amulets displayed in glass cases, and other trinkets. "I last saw the scepter after the defeat of his brother, who'd gone evil. That was the day he went neutral, refusing to be part of the fight anymore."

"How can you be sure he still has it?" Elisa asked, pausing in her search.

"Ali Baba?" Red scoffed. "He's never lost a single item, aside from this dagger."

"And now he'll be having that dagger back," a voice said. One of the suits of armor stepped forward, sword raised.

I was closest to the armor, and had my sword at the ready, so went to meet it. The armor was quick, thrusting and cleaving, and even with Red joining in and darting about as she did, it was hard to keep this bastard at bay.

When the doors burst open, a man and woman rushed in with pistols drawn. The woman, who I assumed must be Morigana, wore a scarf over her head, her clothes bright and flashy. The man had a darker, more thuggish look about him and looked too young to be Ali Baba so I figured it must be his son. Hekate flung out her hands and the shots that came from those pistols went flying left into the hallway walls, and then Sharon was pouncing, engaging the man and knocking his pistol to the ground. Red went for the woman in a flash, cloak blocking my view for a moment, but I was still busy fighting the suit of armor anyway.

When Pucky joined me, I managed to step back and catch my breath, and saw that Morgiana was actually holding her own against Red. The man, however, was having a harder time with Sharon, who was half-wolf at that point.

Pucky backed the armor into a corner and fired a point-blank blast from her rifle. The shot dented part of the armor to the extent that anyone in there would've been dead.

But it still kept fighting.

"He's not in there," Pucky said as she stepped back, parrying a blow with her rifle.

At first I didn't register what she'd said, but then I noticed a movement in the reflection from a nearby mirror—not movement of a person, but of a shadow. I spun and grabbed a lamp, lifting it to lug it in the direction of the shadow, when a voice shouted, "No, not the lamp!"

Everyone froze, staring at the spot as a hat was lifted and placed on an invisible head.

"Who are you?" the voice demanded.

"Myths," Elisa replied, standing with hands at the ready. "And you must be Ali Baba himself?"

There was a brief silence, and then he said, "Ah, yes. I nodded, forgot that I was invisible. You're here to steal from me, but you claim you're Myths. Explain yourselves."

"Don't bother, father," the man in the hallway said, at that moment pinned to the floor by Sharon in wolf form. "Last I checked, this is the Big Bad Wolf, and she's no Myth."

"She is now," I said, and when they all turned to me, a gasp came from the direction of Ali Baba. A glance down and I saw that my sword was shining as if in response to their challenge of our Myth status.

"That… the sword… Excalibur?"

I held it high. "It is."

"And how did you come about it? More importantly… would you be willing to make a trade? Anything but the scepter."

"None of your business, and no."

"Then we have nothing to discuss."

"You're invisible," Elisa said, stepping forward now and lowering her hands. "I'm going to make the assumption that it was done via a curse. Maybe some item you have here?"

Silence.

"What if I told you we could break your curse?" Elisa went on. "Would that be worth the scepter to you?"

"You… can do this?" The hope in his voice gave him away.

"Do we have a deal?" She thrust out her hand toward the hat, and a second later the hat was next to her, her hand moving up and down.

"You break this curse, and as much as I hate to part with such a valuable item… it's yours."

"This will hurt," Elisa said, and motioned to me. "Sorry, but we'll be needing that shirt."

I handed it over, figuring this was a worthy cause. She told him to put it on, after warning him that it would hurt, but he still screamed in agony as he tried.

Morgiana threw Red aside and took a step forward, about to attack.

"Morgiana, no," Ali Baba said, and he was starting to become visible. This man was weathered, and I imagined he'd seen better days. Still, when he turned to the mirror and laughed, touching his face to be sure it was really him, he seemed ecstatic to be actually visible, in any form whatever. "They did it, they really did it."

"And you'll hold up your end of the bargain?" I asked him.

"He has no choice," Elisa replied.

"She's right." Ali Baba glanced at Red, frowning. "Though I'd like my knife back. I'll never understand why you took it."

"Long story," Red replied, hand still on the blade. "And… no. It wasn't part of the deal."

Morgiana growled, all glares. "Maybe I take it from her?"

Ali Baba held up a hand and she backed down. The man at her side was staring at Ali Baba, however, and suddenly ran forward, throwing his arms around the older man.

"Father," he cried.

Ali Baba held him close, eyes glistening, and then didn't even look at us as he took a ring from his left hand, turned the stone in it so that lines on the stone matched the lines on the silver. It instantly lit up, matching a pattern on the wall. Ali Baba turned slowly toward it and said in a loud, clear voice, "Open sesame."

The wall slid apart, revealing what appeared to be his most valued possessions, including the scepter —gold, one end expanding out almost like a shovel, and engraved with Egyptian hieroglyphs.

"I take no part in this war," Ali Baba said. "Still, I hope you will remember my contribution here today, for my heart is connected with each piece in my inner chamber."

"Father," his son said, but Ali Baba unclasped him, entered the room, and reached for the scepter. When he returned, he handed it to Elisa, bowed, and then cringed slightly as his hand pulled away.

"He doesn't mean literally, does he?" I asked Hekate, referring to the part about his heart being connected to the scepter.

She gave me an uncertain glance. "It wouldn't be the craziest thing I've ever heard."

I'd read *Harry Potter* too many times to not be very intrigued by this, but when the man turned and told us to go, I realized we weren't going to get answers here today. We had what we'd come for, and now it was time to find this Sekhmet lioness lady, or goddess… or whatever she was.

"Thank you," Elisa said, and she held out the scepter for Hekate. "Thirty minutes or so again?"

Hekate placed a hand on the scepter and instantly shook, her eyes going wide and her face starting to contort into the shape of a lioness. With a flash of purple and black, she was back, shaking as she said, "No, she's calling for it. This will be instant, if you're ready."

"We are."

We all stepped up, ready, and the portal opened.

Morgiana stared after us with interest, but the last image they saw of us was Red giving her the finger.

I rubbed my eyes, trying to see if I was blind or something was covering them, but then fire burst into life, and we could see again. Torches lined the walls of old, tanned stone. An eerie breeze blew past and shadows darted across the floor, some reaching to Sharon and me, pulling at the wolf within. I felt it, and could see the fur growing on her, the wild returning to her eyes.

We'd hoped it was gone with Pan, but apparently we weren't so lucky.

"Where are we?" I asked, glancing over to Hekate.

"My guess, somewhere in Egypt," the witch replied.

We braced for impact, not sure what was coming.

"If she can help us out, she was a famous

Tempest," Elisa said, looking hopeful. "Maybe she can show you a thing or two."

"Not likely," Red countered. "I think I know exactly where we are, and why she's not going to be on friendly terms."

"Go on," Elisa said.

At first I thought that we were in an enclosed room but then I noticed that Red was busy looking into one of the corners and when I focused on it I could see that it wasn't enclosed at all, that in fact there were exit points. Red gestured for us to follow, and indeed, even the torches were blowing in that direction as if telling us which way to go.

"There's a legend," Red said, voice hushed, "based in part on truth. Which parts of the tale are true and which parts are fabricated, I couldn't tell you, but Ra is supposed to have sent Sekhmet to deal with his enemies and she did, but then she couldn't stop. The shadow got her, bloodlust taking over. When they finally caught up with her there were piles and piles of bodies. The legend says Ra poured ten thousand jars of alcohol on her to get her drunk so that she'd stop, though that part would likely be an exaggeration—"

"You think?" Pucky scoffed, but backed off at a look from Red.

"Whatever the case, she was passed out for three days, woken by Ptah—god of creation and fertility at the time—and they fell in love."

"I'm still not making the connection to this place," Sharon admitted.

"This is where the two settled down?" Pucky asked. "Decided they didn't want any more to do with all that?"

"Ptah," Hekate said, shaking her head as she walked next to me. Suddenly she stopped, gasping. "He went dark—I knew him before… Oh, shit."

"What?" I asked.

"She's the one who killed him, isn't she? Her lover."

Red stopped, looked back, and nodded slowly. "Except she didn't exactly kill him. When he went dark, she took him down, trapping his ichor, his soul —in a tomb. I believe we're in that tomb."

"She never left," I said, thinking at once how creepy and how romantic that was.

"She never left," a voice echoed, but it wasn't my own.

We all spun around, searching for the source of that voice. To my horror, everything flashed dark and then was back, but with the walls having moved. Pucky held up her rifle and charged it so that the glow was bright, and Elisa sent out a wave of swan-shaped light that went through the wall in front of us.

"Fakes," she said. "Illusions. Follow me."

I shared a nervous glance with Hekate, as the last thing I wanted to do was walk through walls and not be able to see where I was going. And sure enough, as soon as we stepped through it wasn't at all like the Platform in the Harry Potter movies, but pure darkness and more flashes—only now it was spiraling purple and I could hear a strange whispering in an alien language.

Cold wind blew from our right and a hand on my midsection guided me along. Presumably Pucky, as she'd taken the position directly in front of me. But as we walked my mind filled with doubts, imagining a creature long dead with slimy skin and eyeballs falling out of their sockets.

When the light flashed a moment later, that's exactly what I found—and even felt it clinging to me.

"Shit," Pucky said, only the voice came from the ghoul, and then it was her and the image was gone again, replaced by a glow from her horns and her rifle as darkness otherwise returned.

"Just as I thought," Elisa's voice said from not so far off, though it started to get distant, echoing. "Not illusions so much as playing on our fears."

"So we... ignore everything that happens that could be something we're afraid of?" I asked.

"Try, and my powers can help counter this."

Something moved by my leg, brushing against it so that I nearly jumped. Dammit, my mind instantly went to slithering, monstrous snakes. We kept on, Sharon's hand on my shoulder gripping me tight and breathing quick breaths as she faced her own fears, I imagined.

"Stay with us," Red said. "Whatever they're throwing our way... fuck 'em."

"Elegantly put," Elisa said with a chuckle.

Hearing laughter in a place like this put a smile on my face, the juxtaposition of it with my fear, the sudden switch in emotions, caught me off guard and I was suddenly laughing. I felt crazed, like there was no reason to laugh, yet I couldn't stop.

Then Pucky was laughing too, and it seemed about to catch on when a hissing filled the relative darkness and a shape darted across our path, barely visible in the faint glow.

Elisa sent a burst of light after it, and then it turned, leaping at us and exploding in a flurry of bats and spiders. But we were already past being scared of this place. Elisa's swans emerged, charging forward as Pucky unleashed blasts with her rifle. Red's cloak fluttered out behind her and she darted over to my side as if I needed protection, but Sharon and I stood firm, watching as the barrage vanished.

When the shots and swans faded, so did the darkness.

Only, I was alone. There was an oasis and I found myself standing beside a pond, the ghost of a breeze sending ripples across the surface of the water, and gently blowing through the nearby palms. No sign of the others, no sign of a pyramid or tomb or whatever we'd been inside.

The water rippled again, this time starting to lift. It was cascading off of a head, then a body, as a woman emerged. She stepped toward me, black hair clinging to her dark skin, eyes pure black and skin covered with tattoos but otherwise bare. Her dark nipples stood erect, water trickling down and catching the sun like diamonds as the drops fell back to the water, passing her perfectly curved hips on their way. When she took her next step, the water fell away to give a view of neatly trimmed hair, then her thighs, so smooth and glistening as the water gave way.

She didn't stop walking once she'd exited the water, but came up to me and wrapped one arm around my neck. She was cold—unnaturally so, but my body craved her, begging me to give in to the desires of the flesh.

"You've traveled far to find me," she said, her other hand moving along my chest, up to run a finger along my lips, and then pulling me in for a kiss.

I resisted, putting my hand between us. Sharp pain hit me like a scalding iron and I pulled back to see her tongue darting out like a snake as she stepped back, hands out to her sides and what I now saw to be claws at the ready.

"Pick your next move wisely, or I'll see that it's your last." She blinked and it was like thin layers of membrane covering her eyes.

"You're not Sekhmet," I said, eyeing her.

"That little imp?" The woman let out an evil cackle, then charged me.

I stepped back to block her stroke, my foot sinking into the sand. With a roll I was free, moving as her foot came at me and left a line of black smoke in its wake. When she came at me again, her nude form had a much less tempting appearance as the tattoos lit up and fire burst from her in all directions.

My first thought was the water, so I threw myself back. If the fire hit me, the water could put it out. Except, I realized as I dodged another strike and spun to see large, feathered wings sprout from her back, she'd come from the water. Would my falling in there mean death? Maybe that was her goal, or maybe there'd be more of her within.

I searched for Excalibur to strike back, but the sword was gone! Of course, this was all an illusion, anyway, wasn't it? So it made sense that I'd be unarmed. At least she'd left me clothed.

She had taken to the sky, circling me and shouting how I'd made a mistake, how she was going to tear me limb from limb. But as I searched for a way out—only sand in all directions beyond the palms of the oasis, something caught my eye in the water nearby. I dodged one of her diving strikes and, as she was flying back up to come in for another attack, I leaned out over the water.

Looking out from its depths, deep within and almost invisible, was Pucky. She could've merely been the dark bottom of the water, except for the glow of her horns. Her hand was reaching out to me, the glow reflecting on the sides of her fingers, and I knew what I had to do.

I reached, ready to take her hand. Only, as our fingers seemed about to touch, the reflection of my attacker showed and she was on me, claws digging into my flesh and wings flapping as she pulled me away, cursing and then shouting in an ancient language. Her full body was against me then and I was being pulled up and away from the water.

Contact with her seemed to burn in the way prolonged contact with ice does.

"You're in my head," I said, imagining any power that worked this way was similar to the way fighting darkness worked. As I focused on the joy my ladies brought me and my dedication to my role of being the Protector, I added, "I won't allow it."

And then it was like the water was alive, rising to meet me as I reached for it, and I managed to twist and struggle, breaking the woman's grasp so that I fell and was engulfed in those waters. Pucky was there, grabbing hold of my hand, and pulling me out and free from whatever insanity that place was.

I stumbled, realizing I was standing, and saw that the others were all staring at me with worry, the darkness gone.

"Is he back?" Elisa asked.

Pucky held my hand to hers, kissed it, and nodded as I said, "Yes."

"You scared us there," Red chimed in. "Eyes going all black, talking in an ancient tongue."

I sighed, shaking my head to try and clear it of images of that woman, and then caught sight of her —not her, exactly, but a carving on a pillar. We were in a room with tall pillars, with images of skeleton warriors and the like.

A cat was looking at us with a slight, purple glow.

Before I could point it out or ask if the others had noticed, two blades appeared in thin air in the center of the room. They burst into flames, held by the form of a woman—not the one from my vision—who leaped onto a ledge in front of us. No, not a ledge I saw, but a large sarcophagus.

"You can't have him," she hissed, lifting the blades in a defensive stance. Only then did I see that while her body was certainly that of a woman, her face was that of a lion. There was no doubt we were facing Sekhmet.

"We're not here fo—" Hekate started, but Sekhmet roared and the shadows tore through the chamber, cutting her off and bringing me to my knees.

My head throbbed and my muscles were taut, veins bulging and fur sprouting.

"He calls upon you for help," Sekhmet said, and pointed one of her fiery blades my way. "Your true self will be revealed this night."

I let out a growl while my body transformed, my blade cluttering to the ground, and nearby Sharon was transforming too, while Hekate rose into the air, darkness enveloping her in a spiraling embrace.

"Fight it!" Elisa shouted, but her voice sounded distant, as if through water.

In an explosion of power that sent us off balance, Hekate threw herself at the sarcophagus, thrusting out with her hands so that the top budged slightly. Sharon was at her side a split-second later, in full werewolf form now and fighting, pushing Sekhmet back.

The rest of us were all in a state of confusion, not sure why these two had attacked. What was going on? We weren't here for the being within that sarcophagus. Red was the first to act, tackling Hekate and shouting for her to stop.

Hekate rolled with it, throwing Red off with a burst of magic, then pulling out a blast of fire that Red rebuffed with a flap of her cloak. Now the two were moving around each other in bursts, while Pucky and Elisa went to pull Sharon back.

I wasn't sure where I was needed, but knew that this wasn't right. The confusion in my head was telling me to make five different moves at once, but my gut was saying only that Sekhmet needed to be won over, that the rest of this needed to stop.

Focusing on my inner peace, a clarity swept over me. I reached out and took hold of Excalibur, pushing myself to one knee.

A glow formed from Excalibur, blue and dull, but then I noticed it was coming from beneath my shirt as well. I stood and pulled off my shirt, hastily compressing it and shoving it in my pocket, surprised to see patterns like I'd seen from the sword before on my skin. They were runes and circles, strange designs that glowed stronger as I gained confidence, matching the radiance that was now coming from the sword.

"You're embracing who you're meant to be," Elisa said, and even Sekhmet paused in her assault.

"The shadow was in you…" She growled. "How?"

"This is the newest Protector," Elisa said, moving to throw a blast of white light to halt Hekate's next attack. "Whatever shadow magic you're using here, he'll overcome it."

"Me?" Sekhmet scoffed. "It's the darkness that I'm fighting, that I'm here to protect you all from. And your lies won't divert me from my duty."

"Excalibur has accepted him," Red said, her cloak flashing as she appeared at Sekhmet's side. "You have to see that."

Sekhmet spun, slicing, and Red had to pull back, then again as Hekate attempted an attack on Sekhmet that hit her as a wall of flame. The goddess's eyes lit up and the flames seemed to enter her, emerging from her blades to burn brighter.

"Lies, illusions," Sekhmet said. "It wouldn't be the first time."

Hekate tried a new tactic now, turning at the sight of skeletons in the corner, and I understood why she'd been called the goddess of necromancy. With a flash of her hand the skeletons were up, joining in the fight.

Dammit, this wasn't going as I'd hoped.

Sekhmet came at me again while the others were fighting each other and the skeletons. She pushed me to the wall with a powerful kick, had her tail around one wrist as she turned to plunge one of her blades into my chest. The strike would've gotten me, too, if in that moment Hekate hadn't succeeded in managing to get the lid of the sarcophagus pushed open a bit more.

The motion caused a screeching sound that sent another tremor of darkness through us.

When I blinked, trying to clear my eyes, I wondered at first if I was imagining the spotted cat with purple magic around it, leaping for the sarcophagus. It pounced and the lid moved back slightly into place. A hiss from the cat caused Sekhmet to pull back, to leap up onto the sarcophagus.

I led the attack, this time, not ready to let her kill one of my teammates. She was fighting me off while Pucky used her massive rifle to repeatedly blow the skeletons to bits and occasionally hit Sharon, sending her back, while Red and the cat—who I assumed to be Bastet—fought Hekate.

When Bastet hissed toward Sekhmet, the latter growled back and said, "Kill them now, ask questions later."

Nobody was allowed to talk of killing my friends. Anger at the thought gave me the courage to get in close with Sekhmet, even joining her on the sarcophagus before she managed to slice open my cheek and send me stumbling off.

In a burst of flames she was on me now, pushing me back with strikes that were fast and deadly, but my shield met each of them in turn. My runes glowed brighter with each blow, Excalibur too, and soon it was sparking—as if it was connected to the shield and I was saving up the energy from those strikes. Feeling a surge like I was at the edge of my bursting point, I returned the attack and swung out, thrusting even as I saw her step out of range. Too much power was flowing through me to stop, so I let it go, let it flow through me and into my hands, out through the sword. The light exploded, illuminating the room and knocking the skeletons back so that they fell lifeless to the floor.

Even something about Sekhmet had changed, though I didn't realize what at first. Then I saw that her eyes had stopped glowing, but were staring at me like a normal lioness's eyes would when belonging to a goddess.

"You... you really do have the power." She paused, listening, and then we heard it too—a distant rumbling. "And they sense it now, too."

"They?" I asked.

Hekate spun, paused at a look from Bastet, and then said, "I know."

"Care to fill us in?" Elisa said, standing with hands outspread, all of our eyes darting about, wondering what was happening, what would happen next. Hekate had pressed herself up against a wall, eyes wide, hands trembling, while Sharon was on all fours and back to her human form.

"My sister thinks I shouldn't kill you," Sekhmet said.

"Funny," I said, glancing at the cat but then remembering that maybe they could talk—magic and all.

Sekhmet gave me a confused glance, then motioned to the hall opposite the way we'd come in. "You're Myths? On the side of good and righteousness and all that? Prove it. Your arrival here has unlocked an evil that has been asleep for a long time, though never long enough. See that it doesn't enter this room, and I'll consider not killing you all."

"You'll do us one better," Red said, and for the first time she revealed the scepter.

Sekhmet's eyes went wider and flared green, and for a moment she seemed to lose herself. "Leave it here when you go out to fight. It can't fall into their hands."

"Nor yours," Red replied. "Not until you've agreed to help us find someone for us, you and your sister."

Sekhmet bared her teeth, but the cat at her side stepped forward, eyes intently on Elisa, and then let out a meow.

"My sister would like to hear more," Sekhmet said. "After."

"Am I the only one who wants to know what the fuck happened here?" I asked, then gestured to Sharon and Hekate in turn. "To them?"

"The force within," Sekhmet said, eyes still on the scepter. "It is powerful, calls upon others, brings them to this place. When they are close, it reveals their darkest sides."

I nodded, kneeling next to Sharon and helping her up. "It wasn't your fault."

Sharon's eyes rose to meet mine. "It always is."

"She's right," Hekate said. "The darkness within... we need to fight, to keep it out."

"It's without," Sekhmet said, "like an evil flame that can and must be extinguished.

"What exactly are we fighting here?" I asked.

Sekhmet glanced over at Hekate, disdain in her voice as she said, "You saw what she was capable of, with the skeletons? That, but far worse."

Fighting evil Legends was one thing. Going up against an army of the undead? That freaked me the fuck out.

Still, I held Excalibur at the ready, and nodded. No point in delaying any further.

"Oh, and when this is over," Sekhmet said, leaping off of the sarcophagus and giving me an appraising look, "put your shirt back on. I've been hundreds of years without a man, and the sight of you half-naked is bound to cause some trouble, if you know what I mean."

I stared after her as she exited, quite confused by that remark and even more so by the way she—from the back—looked like a normal, petite and scantily clothed, Egyptian woman. And let's all be honest about the fact that Egyptian women can be damn fine. Damn. Fine. It was a weird thought, knowing that she had the face of a lioness.

Pucky chuckled as she walked by, looking me over too. "You are looking hot," she admitted, and winked.

"I'm not just a piece of meat," I called after them, then stiffened as Red slapped my ass and Sharon and Elisa chuckled.

Maybe I was wrong. Maybe I was just a piece of meat to them—that was fine, because when this was over, I was going to remind them that I was the finest quality meat they'd ever tasted.

But yeah, fighting an undead army first. Yay.

11

I t wasn't until we reached the entrance to another room—much larger and too dark to see the ceiling or far wall, filled with more intricately designed pillars—that Bastet hissed and Sekhmet held up a hand.

"Be wary," she said. "Isis has waged war on me… it's here she'll attack."

"Isis?" I asked, confused. "Wasn't she the goddess of birth or something?"

"Originally, yes—fertility and healing. Until she became corrupt, ran off with my lover and, well…" Sekhmet took a deep breath, lioness eyes flashing in anger as she worked to regain her composure. "It was nasty, the way she'd slaughter others, such as Luasaas, Mut-Shet, and more, to take on their powers and become the monster she is today. She swore an oath to destroy me and absorb my Ichor as well."

"So getting out of here is as much an escape mission for you as it is for us to get you out so you can help track down Morganna?"

She shrugged. "Win-win, as you say."

The cat gave me a curt glance, then moved toward the entrance to the room. She paused, lifting her paw to touch what had been an invisible wall but now shimmered purple and green.

"Are we ready?" Sekhmet asked. "Once we go through this barrier, all hell will break loose."

"Ready," Red said.

Elisa was about to answer, when I raised a hand. "This Isis… Dark hair, covered in tattoos that glow?"

"She can take on many forms," Sekhmet replied, looking at me with curiosity. "But yes, that would be her base form. You've met?"

"Only briefly," I replied with a shudder, noting the knowing look from Pucky. "I'd be just fine never meeting her again."

"I can't promise that, but I'll be sure to tear her throat out first chance I get, if that makes you feel any better."

"Actually," looking at her, I had to admit, "it does."

"Let's get to it then," Elisa said, nodding to Excalibur and reminding me to draw the sword, while the others armed themselves as well.

"If she comes a-knocking, I'll have something for her," Hekate said with a grin, strolling past the rest of us to join the cat, hand up and fire sparking to life from her fingertips.

"Something tells me I'm going to like you bunch," Sekhmet said, and then nodded to Bastet.

The cat pushed her paw through, purple magic of the doorway matching her own, and giving me the impression that the barrier had been of her doing and not the other way around. As the barrier faded, a thud like bass dropping hit, then the pillars began to come to life.

"Quickly now!" Sekhmet roared, and we were charging out.

When I say the pillars came to life, I don't mean they literally did… but the images carved onto them did. Skeleton warriors clad in gold and carrying curved blades leaped out, alongside mummies and winged cats.

Working our way out of the tomb was like shrinking down and charging through a hornet's nest. Dark magic was clearly at work here, and by that I mean the type that had watched too many

Saturday morning cartoons. Armies of skeletons and mummies, bones clattering and groans echoing lurched into view. Spiders and what I had to assume were flesh-eating beetles crawled out of the walls, and this time it wasn't in our minds, no illusions here. Now that Sekhmet and Bastet weren't keeping the darkness at bay, it was throwing all manner of evil at us.

And then we clashed.

First came the skeletons, bones blasting apart or bursting into flames as we hit them with shots and spells. My sword did a number on them, cutting through bone and leaving them writhing on the floor behind us as we progressed.

My arms grew tired as I tore through skeletons and mummies, each swing of Excalibur starting to weigh down on me. Halfway through the room Hekate sent a new wave of snakes and spiders running with walls of flame, but one made it through. I lifted the sword to take a swing, but the energy simply wasn't there. If not for a well-placed shot from Pucky's rifle, which caused the snake's head to explode even as it lunged for me, I would've been in trouble.

I kicked out at a skeleton that came around the next pillar, dodged another's sickle, then came up and threw my weight into a spinning attack that managed to get my sword into position to stop a mostly-decomposed mummy whose unraveling bandages weren't staying on in the slightest.

"That's hardly the worst of it," Sekhmet said, seeing my exhaustion and frowning in frustration. "You're sure you're the Protector?"

"I just started," I confessed moving forward at her side and annoyed that I had to admit to that at a time like this.

She looked slightly worried, but to her credit said nothing more on the subject. At least, not until a line of light coming from a hole in the ceiling was blocked out by a flying form.

"Whatever you know or don't know, it's time to pull up your big boy pants," Sekhmet said. "She's here."

Those wings were clear when passing overhead again, and the flashback of the woman clawing at me in the oasis was enough to give me strength to lift Excalibur. In fact, I realized that her presence—or maybe the fear or excitement of facing her here— was causing my tattoos to glow bright again, and this in turn gave me strength.

Noticing my curious glance down, Elisa took a stance next to me, calling on her brothers so that bursts of light showed first as swans, then three of her brothers in shining armor of blinding light took up the defense, fighting the skeletons and other forces to give us some room.

"When true darkness is close, your light shines through," Elisa explained. "In a way it's a sign of danger, because you'd only need the extra strength to face true evil, but hey—better to have the extra burst than not."

"Damn straight," I said, adjusting my grip on the sword and watching for any signs of Isis coming back in for a strike.

A gush of wind came first and I thought it was her until two women attacked—one missing half a jaw, both with eyes eaten out long ago and wearing what would've otherwise been sexy, gold Egyptian jewelry and very little clothing. Watching mummy movies I'd always known there was a hot actress underneath the makeup, making even these scenes hot. Let me tell you right now that the reality is quite different. Even when one of their breasts fell out during an attack, nipple almost hitting me in the face, it was probably the farthest from "hot" I could imagine. These long-dead ladies were reanimated corpses fighting on the side of my enemies.

Yeah, not hot.

I thrust with Excalibur only to be blocked by

their curved blades, very similar to Sekhmet's. One went for a leg sweep and I went down, totally caught off-guard by how fast they were.

Flashing flames cut through one of them, leaving a writhing corpse on the ground, and I looked up to see Sekhmet going for the other. She glanced over and simply pointed behind me while preparing a strike.

When I spun around, I was face to face with Isis. She'd just struck Pucky, who now had three of these dead-women minions on her.

A clawed hand came for my throat but I swung upward with Excalibur and caught her—not hard enough, as the blade stuck in her flesh and stopped on bone. Shit, how hard did people swing these things to be able to cut an arm off? She roared and lunged, pinning me down with the blade still in her, my team and our recent additions fighting off the other monsters in all directions and unable to come to my aid.

It was time to prove I could carry my weight. Hell, I still wondered what made me so special anyway. What was it about being a Protector that gave me any advantage in a fight that, say, Jean-Claude wouldn't have? I certainly couldn't do spinning jump kicks like he could. But I had this sword, and some strange glowing tattoos... that had to mean something.

I pushed back, focusing my energy into the light and away from sheer force, and my tattoos glowed brighter—so bright, in fact, that Isis had to pull back to cover her eyes. That gave me the moment I needed to roll out from under her and regain my sword.

One massive swing of Excalibur and I had the rest of her arm off! I was going for the neck, but she managed to throw her remaining arm up in a blocking motion. But this wasn't some ordinary Legend, this was a goddess who had taken others' powers into her own, and so it made sense on some strange level when her blood splattered out into shapes of mini-demons that started in on me.

My sword was of light, pure, so it cut them down, but I was backing away as she recovered and flew into the sky, hand outstretched and eyes turning to flames. The room spun and the flames and bursts of light and skeletons were all a blur of darkness and blotches of colors. She was trying to pull me back to the spirit realm, the Fae land.

Since she had an advantage there, I wasn't having it.

"No!" I shouted, swiping with Excalibur, and then I was charging in the direction of the flapping of her wings, swiping to try and hit more of those demons as I went. One spot of brightness became viewable in that moment—my screen saying I'd leveled up to five, though no new Ichor points to assign. I'd take what I could get.

Darkness surrounded me and my last step sent me falling into nothingess—except that my sword caught her, or something, and it was like a climbing hold stuck into the side of a mountain as I clung on desperately, my only means of not falling.

Her shrieks echoed above all other sounds, and she flapped, rising high with me attached. My vision returned as she lost focus, and I saw two of the swan brothers running toward the spot I had been, directly below me now. Knowing what I had to do, I grabbed my sword with both hands, flung my legs up, and kicked out. The blade came free and I fell…

Caught by the two brothers as they flew up, partially shifted between swan and human. We were soon on the ground again and running. I realized my team was ahead of us, Hekate and the other newcomers taking up the rear.

"Get out of here!" Sekhmet said, motioning as she slid across the ground, fiery blades cutting through a sphinx and setting it aflame.

I did as she commanded, no questions asked. More dark forms appeared in our path, Shades and several men with the heads of dogs, but we made mincemeat out of them and were through. Turning, I saw Sekhmet go full lioness mode, tearing through one more of them and then leaping to meet Isis mid-air—the two pummeled down as Bastet made it through the doorway, and then Sekhmet was right behind her.

Isis was up and coming in fast, Sekhmet leaping and Bastet hissing. A clawed hand reached out for Sekhmet's tail, and then Sekhmet was on our side, Bastet letting out a sound like a high-pitched meow. Isis slammed up against a translucent purple barrier.

She stood glaring at us, blood still dripping from her one arm, and opening her mouth to yell—but no sound made it through.

"She's trapped," Sekhmet said, returning to her humanoid form with the lion face. "That barrier will hold her... for now. She's not strong enough to break out on her own."

I turned, pulling up my screen to quickly assign my new prana, but just as I was finishing Elisa said, "We're not done yet."

Sure enough, more of those monsters—the men with dog faces, some wearing loincloths, others hanging out for the world to see—were approaching. I closed my screen and charged, no hesitation in this moment. The last thing I wanted was for Isis to somehow break out of there.

"Weaken them," Hekate said, "but keep as many alive as possible."

"You're not making sense!" I shouted, already stabbing through a mummy with my sword and then kicking it off.

"Just do it!"

I growled, backing off and working on disarming them instead, making non-lethal strikes when possible, while the others worked their magic.

"Now!" Hekate said, and she stepped forward with hands extended. Green tendrils shot out into the surrounding throng of monsters.

"You fight for me now!" she declared, and then pulled. Sure enough, the green snapped back, hitting monsters on the way and leaving those of the undead variety with green, glowing eyes. "Attack your brothers and sisters! Destroy those who I have not claimed!"

The skeletons and mummies turned on the others, to the point that the winged beasts and other animals soon tucked tail and fled. We gave chase, Pucky shooting down a good number of them, my prana points coming in hot and fast to the point that I'd just leveled up to six, and Sharon was howling in victory.

It finally calmed down, and Hekate's converted warriors trickled back over to us, where they stood, awaiting their next command.

"We have our army to keep this place under our control," Hekate said. "They'll guard the barrier from this side… at least as long as I'm alive. You're welcome."

"I'm impressed." Elisa stared at her in awe, then turned to Sekhmet. "And you're sure the barrier will hold Isis and… him?"

"I can answer regarding her, but he… let's hope he's not wakened." Sekhmet turned to eye the scepter in Red's hand. "You were saying, about the scepter? I'll have it back… whatever the cost."

"The cost," Red replied, "is that you two help us track down a newly-reborn Legend. King Arthur, to be exact. And Morganna—though she's been absorbed by Riak."

"Mother of Shades," Sekhmet said, sharing a look with the cat. "Yes, we can help you track these two, for the price named."

"How do we know she'll stick to her word?" I asked.

"She's bound to it, for one," Hekate said.

At my questioning look, Elisa explained, "There are certain deals you can't undo without paying a great price. In this case, she'd be impacted by the darkness. It would change her—and while some people can handle a bit of darkness, I have a feeling she's had enough in her life."

The cat curled up around my leg, looking up at me and purring.

"I know," Sekhmet said to the cat, then turned to me. "They're all correct. Being down here as long as I have, and close to… to what was once my lover but is now the farthest thing from love I can think of, has changed me. I have no interest in joining the fight again, but I will not abide in the shadows."

"You'll help us track these two down, then be free to go," Red said. "Agreed?"

"Agreed," Sekhmet said.

Red stepped forward, shook the goddess's hand, and handed over the scepter. Sekhmet sheathed her blades at her back, took the scepter, and held it close as if reunited with a long-lost lover.

"It has a power?" I asked.

"Because of it, I'm able to go with you." Sekhmet lifted the scepter and, as she did so, a shimmer of light passed over her face, transforming her so that—while she still had lioness-like features—she had a woman's face now, and a damn beautiful one at that. Her jade-green eyes stood out even more with the way they were framed by dark eyelashes. This, combined with her smooth skin with high cheekbones made her the epitome of Egyptian goddess.

But she didn't stop there. Turning to the hallway, she stretched out her arm with the scepter as if it was an extension of her arm, and a ray of light shot out, filling the hall until it was as if glowing stones paved the way.

"If anyone makes it past our little army out there, courtesy of the witch, well…" Sekhmet grinned, indicating her handiwork. "They'll have to find a way through this, and that would take some powerful magic indeed." She paused for a moment, glancing over. "You don't happen to have my sun disk, do you?"

"Not yet," Elisa said with a wink.

At the 'yet' part of it, Sekhmet looked very intrigued.

"Now what?" I asked.

"Now," Sekhmet replied, turning to me and holding out an arm for the cat to leap into. "We track down some evil reborn Legends."

The sparkle in her eyes told me that, as much as she'd been against fighting in this war, the thrill of the fight was alive within her.

"And put on your shirt already," she added with a laugh. "I'm sure your ladies would hate if I tore off the rest of your clothes and took you right here, but I'm damn close to doing so. Damn close."

She turned and started walking, leaving the rest of us to stand there awkwardly for a moment, processing that.

"Oh, right," I stammered as I tugged my shirt out of my pocket and dressed as I ran to catch up.

12

Our first goal was to get out of Egypt, but only when we had a destination. Our first step on that journey was to find a town with a railway station and that meant trudging across the desert at night, freezing if not for the warmth of the light Sekhmet cast upon us with her scepter. If she had the disc, she told us, we wouldn't even notice the chill on the air.

"Before, when you said going dark was like being in a dream," Sharon started walking closer to me, eyes looking lost in thought, "I don't know. I've been thinking about it, and I don't think that's right. Not for those of us who've been there longer, or those who don't know the difference. Some were born into darkness and have never left it. Imagine, if you will, being born into a 'dream' and not knowing what reality is. For many, it's like that—they don't know what's considered just, or right, and the idea of doing anything other than what you've been raised to do seems impossible."

"I get it," Pucky said, walking up on the other side of Sharon and wrapping an arm around her, too. "My sister fell to the darkness. I've tasted it, and come back."

"Will…" I started. "I mean, do you think Riak's able to?"

"Come back?" Pucky stared out at the night, at the silhouette of Hekate where she walked slightly ahead of us. "I think she could, but don't think she will. The problem is…" She glanced over to Hekate, and then Sharon. "It's tough, once you've crossed certain lines."

Sharon cleared her throat, Hekate glancing back with a look of contempt.

"What, you want a list of our transgressions?" the witch asked. "Because fuck that."

"Of course not," Pucky replied. "I was simply—"

"Simply judging us for the wrongs of our past," Sharon said, but then held up a hand to Hekate. "And there's nothing wrong with that. We've done what we've done, regardless of how we were externally influenced. And be honest, at times you embraced the darkness—you more than most, perhaps."

Hekate shrugged, looking smug in the thought, and then nodded. "I'm a murderous bitch, but now I'm your murderous bitch. Doing 'horrible things' in a war is only horrible when done by or for the other side, no?"

"No," I said, finally taking a stance. "Someone in war can torture, and it's wrong. You can attack innocents, kill children to scare off your enemy. Wrong. Killing someone when taking them prisoner is an option? Wrong, ninety-nine percent of the time. But you're right, you're on our side now, and my thought on that is it's awesome—but only if you're going to do it the right way."

Hekate looked affronted, but Sharon was smiling, as if I'd just said the most brilliant thing ever. I worried about Chris going off with the witch, but figured Elisa knew what she was doing if she was pairing them up. Or hoped she did, anyway.

We kept walking, changing the discussion to more about strategy, how we were going to use our various skills to attack when we found Morganna, and how Arthur might have more vampires at the ready to face us. I asked about garlic and stakes and all that, expecting them to laugh, but Elisa simply nodded and said, "They're in stories because we put them there. We have to prepare you Normies somehow."

It was almost morning by the time we reached a small town with a train station, and by then I was more than ready to pass out. The village wasn't more than a few dozen buildings, most looking like shacks and some with gates made straight out of the ground. A couple of people gave us weird looks but kept walking, and I remembered that Red's cloak worked to keep us seen in the way we wanted to be seen, and Pucky's horns weren't visible to others. It was likely a safe assumption that they weren't seeing Hekate as a witch or Sekhmet as their lion goddess or whatever she was either.

Sekhmet explained that Bastet would need time to do her tracking ritual. Luckily we found someone who, on seeing who wanted it, agreed to rent out their house to us. They vacated and went to stay with a neighbor while we took possession. Once inside I took a few steps, appreciating the simplicity of the mud-brick design, then saw a bed, dropped onto it, and promptly passed out.

It was still very early morning when I woke, the moon still in the sky though moving closer to the dunes in the distance, stars sparkling overhead like I'd never seen them in my life. A warm breeze ruffled my hair and I stood there for a moment, enjoying it, before walking on. Two more steps and I had to pause to stretch my back. The pile of blankets and hard pillow weren't exactly what I was used to, but at least we'd had a bed instead of the train car I'd expected when we reached here.

I got up and went out to the courtyard where I knew Bastet had been working, but found her still at it, moving about as Sekhmet performed a sort of meditation, sitting still as could be, her face that of a lioness again and glowing slightly. Patterns had formed on the ground, indicating the level of magic this whole situation took to accomplish.

Not wanting to interrupt, I made my way back toward the bed but noticed Pucky standing in the hall by the front step. As I approached, I saw that she was watching a form on the steps.

"What's going on?" I whispered, stepping up next to her.

She looked startled to see me but then smiled, took my hand, and gave it a reassuring squeeze. "It's Sharon. She's been sitting out there for over an hour. I'm… worried."

I frowned, then moved up next to Sharon and sat, Pucky coming a moment later and sitting on the opposite side.

For a moment, we all sat in silence until finally, without even a sign of having seen us, Sharon said, "I've just been staring at the stars—lights in the darkness, right? Like me, now… like us."

"Wouldn't you say it's more like the Legends are small patches of darkness in a world of light?" I asked.

"Maybe…." She finally looked at me, pensively, then turned to Pucky and nodded before looking back out at the sky. "Depends where you put humanity on that scale, I suppose."

"That's the difference between Myths and Legends," Pucky explained, upon seeing my confusion. "Legends see humans as a parasite on this earth, or as a disease that needs to be eradicated."

"And you don't?" Sharon countered.

"We tend to think of them as more like self-destructive cute little bunnies."

"Excuse me?" I scoffed, not sure if she was joking.

"You can't deny that humanity is responsible for putting our planet on this trajectory toward ruin," Pucky said. "Myths see it as our role to protect humanity from itself… and from the Legends."

Sharon sighed. "I'm trying to come around to that way of thinking… but it'll take time. You're hunted by agents so long… your worldview becomes jaded."

"You're not alone there," Pucky said.

"Yeah?" Sharon turned to her, then me, a hint of a smile at the corner of her lips. "Without you two, I don't know what I'd do. Thank you."

She turned back to the stars, resting her forearms on her legs.

Pucky leaned back, making eye contact with me, and gave me a nod. I shrugged, not sure what that was for. She motioned this time with a nod toward Sharon, still leaning forward between us. I frowned, not getting it, so this time Pucky puckered her lips, then started moving her tongue as if frenching someone.

She wanted me to make a move on Sharon! I blinked, confused, but she took my hand and started rubbing it up and down Sharon's back. A moan escaped Sharon, and when she looked up at me, it was clear her mind was in the same place as Pucky's.

Fuck it.

I leaned in, gently caressing the side of her face with my hand, and ran my lips across hers. It was a brief kiss, a tender one to test her, to see if she was ready. When I pulled away, she came back in for more—definitely ready. Now her lips were pressed firmly to mine, her tongue tasting me and teasing, having fun with it.

When she came up for a breath and smiled, she went rigid as Pucky's hand found her chin, guiding her back around, and then Pucky leaned in and kissed her too.

Sharon didn't react at first. Her back straight, her

hands frozen where they'd been on me. But then she started moving her head, one hand on my leg, the other accepting Pucky's, the two moving their fingers along each other's as if making love.

I had to admit, it was hot.

"This is an every time thing?" Red said, and we turned to see her standing there, cloak whipping about in the wind. "Her?"

Sharon pulled away, then stood to leave.

"Wait," I said, and stood too. "You certainly didn't have a problem last time."

"My… lust took over," Red countered.

"What is it you have against her? I mean, aside from your fairy tale history—"

"Which isn't really even history," Pucky pointed out, leaning back and still breathing heavily. "Don't forget, Sharon's not the original."

Red frowned. "Of course."

"So…?" Pucky persisted, and Sharon was looking at Red now, curious.

"I… I'm not sure," Red admitted. "Maybe it's just that—maybe it's an association with the original. I don't know—but that doesn't mean I have to like it."

Pucky stood, shrugged, and walked over to Sharon, taking her hand and placing it over her heart, just at the edge of the top of her breast, exposed by a low-cut shirt. "But you can give her a chance."

Red arched an eyebrow, then turned to me, waiting to see what I would do.

"Me?" I asked, then glanced between her and Pucky. "We have our team. I wouldn't do anything to jeopardize that, and if you don't feel comfortable here… Well, I think it's worth having a conversation about."

"A conversation?" Red's frown was replaced with worry. She took a step to leave, looked back at Sharon's hand resting awkwardly at the top of Pucky's breast, and said, "Well, if Sharon thinks she's ready now, and we're going to truly indoctrinate her, don't you think we should… I don't know, do it somewhere more formal?"

"And invite Elisa," Pucky said, wrapping her arms around Sharon's waist and pulling her close. "Yeah?"

Now Sharon was starting to look slightly over-whelmed, but she nodded. "If you all say so. I mean, I'd hate to impose."

I laughed, totally not having expected it to take this turn, but not fighting it. We got up and went inside, where we found Elisa waiting for us. It was interesting to see that Sharon turned to Red, already expecting it to be like last time. The latter blushed, then smiled, and stepped forward to start kissing her, the two running their hands over each other. This was a team, and I liked the way our teamwork and sharing was going. If all the talk of getting down hadn't already gotten me hard, this would've.

When Sharon started taking control, the first to slide a hand up Red's skirt, it got even more interesting. But I wasn't here just for a show, so I turned to see Pucky and Elisa both standing there, watching me with seductive grins, waiting.

I wasn't sure where to start, still thinking I might offend them if I went with one over the other, so I simply stepped forward. They stepped closer, pulling me between them, both kissing my neck, undressing me, caressing my chest, my ass, my cock.

We were all naked then. Pucky's lips found mine, her tongue teasing me, and then it was Elisa, and then they were kissing each other, hands still on me.

"You like watching?" Elisa asked, pulling away from the kiss to nibble at my ear.

At my noncommittal shrug, she guided a nervous-looking Pucky over to the bed, had her kneel, and then laid back with her head between Pucky's legs so that she could eat her out, legs spread to show exactly what she had in mind.

I took up position and teased the edge of Elisa's pussy with my cock, Pucky breathing deep and running her hands along first her breasts, then down to Elisa's as she watched me.

Elisa's tongue was flicking out, then lapping at Pucky, and the latter was having a hard time staying up, reaching for the wall and moaning. Not wasting any more time, I took my cock by the base and guided it in. Elisa was warm, moist, and when I saw that all three of the women were watching me while touching themselves and each other, it gave me another boost of arousal.

Fucking Elisa this time had a whole new feel to it. When Pucky and I leaned forward to kiss while it was happening, her biting me as pleasure hit her, I was on fire. Literally, I noticed—blue flames burning from my tattoos.

Pucky yelped, falling back off of Elisa's face, and even I started, so that I slipped out. All three women were staring at me.

But it didn't hurt, and now that I'd stopped, so did the flames.

"What the hell…?" Red said, stepping close. She pushed me onto the bed, considered me a moment, and then grabbed my cock, stroking it. I leaned back, breathing out a low moan, and heard her muttering something under her breath. When I looked, the flames were back and she had a hand held up, turning circles of green light in the air.

My eyes must have betrayed my fright, because she let the green light go and smiled. "It's perfectly safe, and…" Taking her free hand, she moved her fingers through the small blue flames, a tremor passing through her body. "As I expected. It's not fire —more like the Eternal Flame, an old fire that holds many stories."

Elisa approached now, running her hands along me, enjoying it now too. "He's connecting with the spirit realm, through… sex?"

They all looked at Pucky, who had her hands wrapped around her midsection, still looking at me with worry. At their stares, though, she approached, hesitantly. Gently moving Red's hand aside, Pucky pulled me on top of her, our flesh held together, and her eyes took on the blue of the flame, glowing the same way it did.

"Enter me," she said, and her voice sounded like it was coming from somewhere else. I did, and the flames engulfed the two of us with such ferocity that the others leaped back and Sharon cursed. All of that came second, though, because suddenly Pucky and I were rocking in and out of our world with each thrust, the flames flaring as our surroundings were replaced by vast oceans, waves taking us and crashing against our flesh—all of it warmth and pleasure. We were floating as the fire turned to water, then we were in the sky, the winds caressing us as we made love, and I grasped her by the back of the head, pulling her into a passionate kiss that I never wanted to end.

When she came, she reached out to her left and right, and suddenly Elisa and Red were there, a moment later Sharon appearing, too, and while they all looked scared and overwhelmed, they soon joined in. If I'd been high on ecstasy and acid in the middle of a whorehouse, I imagine it would've been similar to this experience, except this was real and it didn't have that out-of-body, hallucination effect drugs caused (so I hear). This was real, and I was going from one to the other, pulling them close, feeling myself inside them as if we were one, and then experiencing their orgasms along with them.

Finally it was Red's turn, and she pressed her pussy tight against my cock, moaning and holding my face, staring into my eyes. She bit her lip, shaking her head.

"Still?" I asked.

She kissed my forehead and said, "Soon, but not yet," and then lowered herself, floating through the sky, to take me in her mouth while the others caressed me and her.

I didn't last much longer, not with all of that ecstasy surrounding me and the beautiful women so pleased, their emotions and satisfaction still flowing through me. It hit like a tidal wave flowing up and out of the ocean, the sensation of my orgasm. I opened my mouth to warn her, to give her the chance to move her mouth, but she was caressing me and sucking away, so into it I doubt she would've heard me anyway, and then it was happening before I could even process it.

Blast after blast of pleasure rocked me, my hips thrusting out and my hands suddenly gripping her by the hair, overwhelmed by it all, moaning and then letting out a long, "Ahhh," before finally letting loose, going limp.

We were back in the room, Red with a hand to her mouth, clearly trying to swallow, but it was too much, and she had to hold up a hand and go running out of there.

"Oh," a voice exclaimed from the hallway, and then there was the sound of spitting from the bathroom, followed by gentle laughter from Pucky.

When Red returned, she looked at me with wide eyes. "You could've killed me!"

Now Pucky's laughter wasn't held back, and Elisa even joined in with a chuckle. Sharon looked legitimately worried.

"Can that happen?" Sharon asked. "I mean, I guess, but…"

"Of course," Red shot back. "I could've choked, or drowned, I don't know. Holy shit," but she was smiling, "that was a lot of fucking cum."

"It was intense," Elisa said, running a hand along my chest, tracing one of the blue tattoos—no longer in flames.

"I'm—sorry?" I offered.

"Don't be," Red replied, coming back over to me and sitting at my side, a hand on my thigh. She was staring at me with wonder. Then she turned to Pucky. "Explain."

"As I said." Pucky shrugged. "And as I think you all saw—it's like our intimacy with him helped connect him to the spirit realm—connect all of us, actually."

"Even me," Sharon said, her voice full of awe.

"Why wouldn't it?" I asked.

Sharon looked away, and my eyes roamed over her beautiful body as she stood, going to the wall. She stared out the small window, moonlight falling upon her breasts. "I know in my mind I'm with you all, but… part of me wondered."

"If the shadow was still in charge?" Pucky asked, knowingly.

"Exactly." Sharon turned, eyes full of hope. "But after that, I don't know, it's like I don't have doubts anymore. Like, as long as I'm with you all, there's no way the shadow can ever take me again. I'm my own woman."

"That's the thing about light," Elisa said. "When it's complete, when your whole heart is lit, where can the darkness hide?"

Red frowned at her, then scoffed. "Oh my gods, enough with that enlightenment shit. Point is, Sharon, you got a good fuck. That's all the enlightenment you need."

We all had a good laugh at that, but then Sharon said, "No, I mean—yes, it was good—but I agree with Elisa. It's more than that."

Red shrugged.

"And on that note." Pucky turned to Red in confusion. "Why're you still holding out?"

"It's okay," I said, seeing hesitation in Red's gaze. "I get it."

"Do you?" Pucky scoffed. "I sure as hell don't."

"I'm—trying something new," Red explained. "Trying to approach all this differently from the past."

"For the first time, she wants it to mean something," Elisa said, nodding to show she got it. "Good for you, Red. But don't wait too long—at the rate we're going, we might end up fucking the Protector to death and then—"

"Not funny," I interrupted her. "Sometimes I think you're damn close to actually doing so."

Elisa chuckled, shrugged, and said, "Don't worry, we could find a way to bring you back. Probably."

It was my turn to frown, but she winked, then stood to get dressed.

"When it's time," Pucky said, slapping Red playfully on the ass, "make sure we're there. I want to see the look on your face when he slides that gorgeous cock into your pussy after it tightens up from all this non-use."

Red punched her playfully, an act that caused her still-bare breasts to shake and turn me on. Of course, it probably was enflamed by the fact that now I was imagining what our first time would be like.

She saw me staring, pursed her lips, then said, "Pervert" while jokingly covering herself and standing to get dressed.

"Is that even a thing?" I asked, dressing along with the rest of them. "I mean, could I be a pervert for looking, after what we just did?"

"You're safe," Sharon said, and then pulled at my pants before I had them up, to get another look at me. "See? Not perverted."

I laughed, enjoying this more playful side of her.

When we were dressed again and met in the courtyard, Hekate was there staring off at the moon in the early morning sky. Purple lined the dunes in the distance, turning to dark blue above then shading to pink.

"You miss him, don't you?" Pucky asked, teasingly.

Hekate grinned. "I heard you all in there... made me think of him is all."

"And you're right," Elisa chimed in. "It's time to get you started, so that doesn't fall behind. You can make your way back to him?"

"Always."

With that, she said her farewells and found a secluded spot to make a new portal form. Before long, we were watching her step through it, on her way to join Chris and go to fulfill their mission together. Mowgli would be there to show them the way, set it all up. I looked forward to one day returning to hear all about it.

After Bastet finished her tracking spell, we were all eager to be on our way. After exchanging money at a horrible rate, we bought our train tickets and for some meat in baked bread for the journey. We ate those while the train started off, and before long were able to relax, enjoying our full bellies and recent victory.

But man was it slow.

The train felt like an endless journey compared to the speed of travel with portals, but I supposed magic was spoiling me in more ways than one. When I asked again about portals and why that wasn't an option, Sekhmet explained it would mess with their tracking magic, though I thought I remembered something about how witch portals worked and it not being possible here anyway.

There was no dining car, but a grungy old man selling candies and what reminded me of tacos but were made with fluffy dough. Around lunch time we bought some of the latter and it was delicious, grease dripping down my chin as I gobbled the meat and dough up. Not quite as good as the ones we'd bought back at the village, but still damn good. Considering that travel like this had until recently been completely outside of my concept of reality, it was almost as unrealistic as the fact that I'd recently gotten a blowjob from Red Riding Hood or slept with the Swan Princess. Both very strange concepts in themselves, but here I was in actual Egypt!

Straining my eyes to catch a glimpse around, all I saw was desert and the small towns we passed through. It continued on like this, with the most interesting sight aside from sand being the way several sheep were hung and gutted along the side of the street, viewable from the train when it stopped to take on several new passengers.

As I leaned back to finally get some sleep, I noticed Sekhmet eyeing me while Sharon and Pucky slept. Red was on lookout, while Elisa was petting Bastet (a weird action, I thought, considering the fact that the cat was actually Sekhmet's sister).

"Hoping to see the pyramids?" Sekhmet asked.

I shrugged in response, but then muttered, "We're all the way here…"

"Unfortunately, we won't. If we caught a bus, it would be easy enough. But something tells me we're not here for tourism."

"That something being me," Elisa said, glancing up from the cat.

Sekhmet smiled. That was a nice look on her, when her face was in human form like at that moment. "They're truly breathtaking, though there are many sights here unknown to most Normies much more awe-inspiring. If we ever get a chance to return, I'll show you." My heart sank, and apparently my face showed it, because she laughed.

"Don't forget we have other ways to travel," Elisa said. "Or will once Hekate and Chris are successful. I'm not sure how long Sekhmet will be sticking around, but… you having time to do a bit of sight-seeing after this Morganna issue is dealt with could be a real possibility."

I was sitting up again, wondering how travel via portals would work with sightseeing, and the many places we could go. It wasn't as awesome as my first thoughts made it seem, though, I had to remind myself, because the portals could only be currently existing ones—which might be occupied by dark forces—or made to areas where an object came from. At least, that was my understanding. Then again, maybe there were ways around it? I looked forward to finding out more, and lay back, day dreaming about going to the pyramids, the temples of Japan, the Coliseum in Rome, and more, as my eyes eventually closed and sleep took me.

"Careful now," a voice said, and I opened my eyes to find Sekhmet kneeling between the seats, a hand on my knee, a finger to her lips. It was dark outside, a chill coming through a partially opened window in the back of the car.

I thought she was about to go down on me on the train, an idea that had a very high level of appeal, but considering my recent bouts of sexual activity was honestly a bit intimidating. It wasn't like I had superpowers or a dick that could go over and over and heal itself between rounds or something.

Only, then it became clear she was gesturing over her shoulder with a movement of her eyes, and the other ladies were awake too—nobody moving, but everyone alert.

"What is it?" I asked in a whisper.

"Something that boarded at the last stop, I think," Sekhmet replied. "My sister picked up on it first, and now Elisa senses it, too. Also," she gestured at my shirt.

I looked down to see that, sure enough, the faint

glow of my tattoos was visible. I'd have to get my jacket back or start wearing more layers. It had only started doing that back at the tomb, and as I was still waking up I had to rack my brain for a moment before remembering that it meant dark forces nearby.

A chill ran up my spine as I imagined Morganna nearby, maybe in the next train car over, waiting to make a move. But waiting for what?

I craned my neck, then heard a clicking. Whatever was there wasn't in the next car, but above us. Moving along the top of our train car. My tattoos glowed brighter, and I reached over to my luggage where Excalibur was concealed, and gripped the handle.

The grinding of brakes sounded a moment later, and to my surprise we ground to a halt in the middle of nowhere. No train stations as far as I could tell in the darkness. No lights or reason for us to be stopping. We sat there for a moment, my heart thudding, and then I actually jumped slightly as the door to our car opened. A man entered, beady little eyes darting my way before he turned and took a seat.

It didn't make sense.

I nudged Pucky and said, "What're the chances Morganna would know where we are?"

"Since your sword is traceable, I'd say pretty

good." She shifted, trying to get a glimpse of the man who'd entered. "They're putting the chess pieces into play."

"My thoughts exactly," Sekhmet replied, "though chess isn't where my mind went."

"Stay seated," the man's voice came, low and calm. "When they strike, let me act first."

This was getting weirder by the second. Sekhmet turned to each of us, likely trying to see if we knew that voice, but we were all equally confused. Or at least, I thought as much until Pucky's eyes went wide and she muttered, "VH?"

"Patience," the voice replied. "Wait for them to strike."

I was racking my mind to try and remember if I'd heard anything about a man who might go by the initials VH, but got nothing other than old references to the VHS tapes my dad had always talked about.

Before anyone had a chance to ask, however, a window burst in and a grey monster followed. Its eyes were red, fangs protruding like a vampire—in fact, I saw as it lunged for me that it had to be exactly that. It was nude other than its skin clinging to its bones, but such a monster that it didn't seem odd. Its claws stretched out, growing longer the closer it came.

My sword was up before it could hit, but there wasn't enough space for a good blow. Instead I managed to thrust into its gut while the man ahead stood and turned, shooting a rapid succession of what had to be silver spikes. One hit the vampire and it exploded into dust and blood, burning up as two more were hit behind me—these two being among several that I hadn't realized had boarded. The ladies were up and turning to fight, but this VH person was taking control, sliding through between seats and pulling more of those silver stakes to attack, thrusting and stabbing and taking out more of those vampire bastards.

"Oh shit," I said aloud, making eye contact with Pucky. "Arthur—here?"

Her eyes went wide at the thought and she was up, shouting, "Off the train so they can't corner us."

VH seemed to agree, along with Elisa, as we all made for the door while Sekhmet and the cat made a barrier behind us and Red went to the front of the car to check that others weren't being hurt.

It wasn't until we were off the train that I noticed the spiraling black and purple in the sky off in the distance, a silhouette of a woman with curved horns hovering there.

"Morganna," Elisa said, and immediately diverted her attack from the vampires—of which more were closing in on us, but this VH guy was doing a great job of dealing with. Elisa thrust out and called upon her swan brothers again, first with a burst of light that caused Morganna to have to dodge, then with a spinning attack she was surrounded by the three brothers in white, like ghosts moving through the vampires, striking and tearing them down. A flash of fire followed, and Sekhmet was in the sky, going for Morganna. Bastet too, glowing purple, hissed and joined the skirmish, so that soon the sky lit up with flashes of purple, red, and orange.

"What group have I stumbled upon?" VH said, grinning at Pucky as she grabbed me by the arm, her horns aglow.

"The type that doesn't take shit," she replied, and then the two of us were moving through the enemy, appearing a second later at the outskirts of the attack so that we could hit them from the rear instead of being surrounded.

She blasted away at a group of them to the left, hitting more that were incoming, and then took a few shots up at Morganna. Why the woman was holding back, I had no idea. What I did know was that the enemy was multiplying—no, not multiplying, I realized as I charged in to attack. Shades were rising from the shadows.

This was great, because now I was getting prana

as I cut them down along with the vampires, and occasional Ichor from the vampires. Apparently, some of them were at Legend level.

It suddenly hit me—VH, fighting vampires…

"Wait, VH for Van Helsing?" I asked Pucky.

She blasted away, grinning, and said, "Not the original, but a great, great grandchild, yeah. Don't tell him, but I always forget his given name for some reason. Hence VH."

"I heard that," VH said, appearing as he leaped over two vampires, twisting to stab them with stakes as he fell. He landed on one knee and then pushed himself up, grinning our way. "But no worries, I'm not even going to ask yours."

I wasn't sure whether to be offended or not, but at the moment I was busy killing Shades and vampires, so the comment was quickly forgotten. My level went up at least four times during that fight —to level nine—and with three Ichor I was starting to feel like the man. Upgrading was going to be fun!

A burst of white light sent Shades evaporating, the swan brothers charging through a group of vampires with Elisa in their wake.

"Can you get to her?" Elisa asked, turning to Pucky.

"Physically?"

"Connect, on the Fae level."

Pucky looked concerned, then glanced my way and held out her hand. "You're coming with me."

I gulped, not sure if I liked the sound of that after my last visit to Fae land, but took her hand and nodded.

A flash of light and our surroundings were replaced with green grass. Intense warriors stood where the Shades had been—now turning to look at us. Black and red armor, but now that I saw closely, there were only shadows in that armor.

Floating above them all, like their goddess, was a woman whose face at one minute had the look of Riak, at another Morganna. Her face was shifting, as if unable to decide which to go with.

She looked at us and floated down, landing a few paces away. "You don't belong here."

"Riak, this is wrong," Pucky replied. "You're in there, and you can still change it all. Undo what you've done."

"And go back to serving the agents? Or worse, you?" Riak's face showed as she laughed, then it flashed back to Morganna. "This will all be over soon enough, child."

"Riak," Pucky tried, but Morganna stepped toward us, the army moving as if attached by chains.

"You've found powerful friends... I can respect

that. But next time I find you, it will be with much more powerful allies at my side."

"Like Arthur?" I said, stepping up as well. "I can't help but ask… where is he?"

Morganna turned her gaze toward me, snarled, and then vanished as the army charged us.

"Out, now!" Pucky said, but before I could reach her, the first of the shadow army had me, grabbing me and continuing to move in, even as Excalibur hacked at them. Pucky shouted and lunged, grabbing my hand as an axe came at us and—

With a THUD we were back in our world, landing on the ground to see more vampire bodies than before, the portal with Morganna closing, and no sign of her.

"Where'd she go?" Red asked, arriving at our side in a flurry of red robes, her magic dagger held at the ready although the enemy was fleeing.

"She's not ready to face me," Sekhmet said, appearing with hands outspread as she walked, pulling dark energy from the fallen vampires. "Not on her own."

"He wasn't there," Elisa noted. "Arthur."

"Nor with Morganna," Pucky said, and I nodded in confirmation.

"King Arthur's risen?" VH asked, kneeling, glaring up at her.

"And you would be?" Elisa asked, glancing from him to Pucky and back. "A friend, or…?"

"Sorry," Pucky said. "I wouldn't call him a friend, exactly, but when it comes to hunting vampires, there's none better."

Elisa nodded, as if that was sufficient, and glanced at the train, looking about to ask if he was coming with, when he took a step away, eyes darting to the retreating vampires.

"I must track them down, finish them off," VH said. "If Arthur's truly risen, he has to be stopped."

"He's not that way, or anywhere close," Sekhmet said. "We have a trace on him."

VH considered her, nodded, and started off after the vampires. "Good luck, then. If you don't kill him, be sure to let him know I'll be along soon enough to finish the job."

We watched him go, then looked around at the chaos. The train conductor was standing at the front of the train, looking our way in confusion, so Red said she'd go take care of him with a bit of magic. Elisa said she'd do the same for any passengers who might've seen anything. Back home others would move in and take care of it, but we were far from home.

"They're able to track the sword?" Sekhmet asked as we boarded the train.

"That's my understanding."

"And yet, Arthur wasn't with them." Sekhmet caught Bastet and took a seat, her sister on her lap, and stared at me with her fierce eyes. "You know what that means, of course?"

"I don't," I admitted.

"Arthur and Morganna... something's not working out between them. My guess is she was here looking for Arthur as much as she was looking for you. Until she finds him, she won't be able to accomplish her primary objective."

"Which is?" I asked.

"She means to unleash the Old Ones," Pucky said, voice low. "Is that what you're saying?"

Sekhmet nodded. "Although, old is relative. I was around before Merlin, before he took the powers of Maleficent and others."

"I'm not following," I said.

"Merlin went evil on us, and it's part of what led Arthur to becoming the vampire he is. A curse, they say. Among powerful magicians, witches, sorcerers and the like, there's a belief that if you absorb enough powers from others of your kind, you can become a truly immortal god—one who can't die, no matter what."

"Has anyone ever achieved it?"

"Not that I'm aware of."

"Me neither," Pucky said, shaking her head and finally, after having checked around, she sat down next to me. She leaned over, head on my shoulder. "Though I hear Merlin had the power of four before he was defeated."

Sekhmet nodded. "And since most people agree that six very powerful ones would be enough, it's a good thing he was finally defeated."

"Defeated by whom?" I asked.

"Actually," Pucky leaned forward to see if Sekhmet had an opinion as she said, "nobody knows."

Sekhmet looked down at the cat, shaking her head. "I had my own problems to deal with, as you saw. I'm afraid I don't have all of the answers on this."

The others were returning then, so I sat back, contemplating what I'd just learned and what that could mean for our situation. Morganna was attempting to become a truly immortal god. That terrified me.

Pulling up my screen I was excited to see where my skill tree could go, aiming for that group attack. Even with three Ichor at once, though, it still wasn't enough. However, what I could do was upgrade the shield to level two, which made it stronger and larger. With my second upgrade I was able to give

Excalibur two boosts, one that was an attachment boost making it lighter and harder to drop; and a second upgrade to amplify my strike, giving it a boost when attacking that momentarily made it sharper and longer.

Both got me closer to my goal of the group Tempest strike, though some other options looked like they'd be great too. Hopefully I had a lot of leveling up to go.

We started off again soon, all of us ready for another break. Before closing my eyes, I pulled up my screen again, looking over my levels and skills. Even though going up against Morganna was a terrifying thought, with powers like this I was starting to feel like quite the badass.

14

We journeyed on for some time, drifting in and out of sleep. We got off the train at the edge of a tourist town well outside of Cairo, where we were able to arrange a flight at a small airfield, thanks to Elisa and her connections (or maybe it was her money).

As the airplane was being prepared, the rest of us found a woman in a corner of the airport with her little, empty restaurant. The metal tables and chairs reminded me of patio furniture, and the section of missing floor that gave way to the dirt beneath didn't inspire confidence in the airport, but when we were seated and served plates of lamb and couscous, I was out of complaints.

"Where exactly are we going?" I asked.

Sekhmet leaned in, motioning me close. "If I told you, others might hear."

"Others meaning… them?" I gestured to my team.

"Funny." She was petting her sister, a fact that I would never get used to. After a moment, she nodded. "Bastet says you can know this, it's—"

"We can see the tickets," Elisa cut in.

Sekhmet frowned, looked down at the tickets in her hand that said, "Milan," and frowned. "Ah, yes, but we shouldn't say it out loud. In case."

I perked up. "Hold on, so we're going to…" I stopped myself, glanced around, and pointed. "For real?"

Her nod was most welcome. Italy was one of the few places in the world I'd always wanted to go, and the idea that I was now getting a free trip—albeit at the cost of having to risk my life to save fairy tales and the world—was pretty fucking awesome.

Judging by Sekhmet's frown, we'd ruined the fun for her. What this told me was that she liked to have fun, and wasn't merely some super old Myth or goddess or whatever. The hint of a smile as she stared at me confirmed it, though it made me curious about what else she was thinking.

"I've been to Europe once," Pucky said, staring off into the skies. "Used to live in Greece for some time, actually—now that's a place where it's no fun to be a

Myth. Legends go crazy over there, though Heracles…" She stopped herself, glancing my way. "Not
that I'd ever go that way," she added, muttering,
"again."

"What?"

"Just a quick makeout session after we took out
that damn Hydra for the twentieth time. In the
corner of an old temple, on a starlit—"

"I get the picture," I said, annoyed that I was
getting annoyed.

"Oh my gods, he's jealous!" Elisa laughed, then
licked her lips. "That's so sweet."

"Who wouldn't be? She's talking about the *actual*
Heracles, right? Hercules, or whatever you want to
call him. I don't think many guys can compete."

Pucky turned to me, very serious, and put a hand
on my knee. "Dear, Jack… You would never have
anything to worry about. He's all muscle—"

"Not helping."

She rolled her eyes. "Women who've lived as long
as we have don't care about how muscular a man is."

"Though, our man is looking sexier lately, you
have to admit," Elisa said.

Red even grinned at this, and nodded.

"I like muscle," Sharon chimed in. "But Heracles-
level muscle? Yuck. It'd be like fucking an animal,
you know?"

"Right." Pucky glared at them. "As I was trying to say, there's a lot more than muscle and horse-cock that we care about. Maybe we've each gone through that phase, but…"

"That big?" Red asked, an eyebrow arched.

Pucky blushed. "Oh, I didn't mean to say that."

"You said it was just a kiss!" Elisa pointed out.

"It was—because he whipped it out. Fuck that. A guy doesn't just whip it out with me unless I ask him to. Fucking animal."

"Are we talking, like…" Red held out her hands, almost a foot apart.

"Oh God." I turned, not wanting to hear this part, especially. While they'd clearly been enjoying me in bed, a foot long was definitely not something I could boast about. Maybe I'd hit seven inches once when I was really, *really* excited, but come on.

"Yeah, about," Pucky said. "But that's when I stepped away. As I said, not a gentleman. Not like you," she squeezed my leg again, and then lifted her hand to my chin and pulled me back to face her. "Don't do that. You're sexy as hell, and me seeing some nasty dick that just happens to be humongous doesn't change a damn thing. You don't think you please me? Fuck that, I know that you know you do. You know?"

"As much as I agree," Red said, "even without

having… tried it on, or in," she shared a chuckle with Elisa, "I have to say the whole insecurity thing is a bit of a bummer. Can we flip that around? Focus on the fact that you have all of us fooling around with you in some form or another, and not a one of us seems to mind?"

Of course she was right, but before I could say so, Sekhmet almost choked on her drink.

"Wait, you're all fucking him?" she asked.

"Well…" Pucky shrugged, and Red couldn't help but smile. Elisa nodded like it wasn't a big deal. I took a sip of my beer, hoping it would hide the fact that I felt totally exposed here.

"And when do I get in on this?"

Now it was my turn to nearly choke. "What?"

Red turned too. "Are you serious?"

"Ten thousand years in a tomb can give you such a crick in the—oh, who am I kidding, it hasn't been that long, but still. I could use a good lay, even if he has a teenie weenie."

I took big chug of my beer.

"Not teeny," Pucky said in my defense.

"A very nice cock, actually," Elisa said. "I've painted it—it's gorgeous."

My eyes went wide, focused on the bubbles in the mug.

"Even better," Sekhmet said. "Where do I sign up?"

"It's kind of a members-only thing," Red explained. "Right now you're our guide, doing so for a price. You join up, become a full-fledged Myth on team Protector, we can talk."

"The boy doesn't speak for himself?"

"The man," I corrected her, "does, but agrees whole-heartedly with my team." Maybe I was feeling emboldened by their nice compliments and coming to the defense of my package, I don't know, but also didn't want to offend her. "Not that it wouldn't be... nice, I imagine. I mean, I wouldn't imagine, because it's not like that—I'm not just a dildo you use whenever you want."

"I'm sorry, I don't get it," Sekhmet admitted.

"It's like a relationship," Pucky said. "Only, we're all involved. And... we kind of have to agree on new parts of the relationship."

"All of you?" Sekhmet turned to Sharon, then Red, knowingly.

"Some of us... took more time to come around," Red answered, and held out a hand, which Sharon stared at for a moment, then kinda high-fived. I was pretty sure that's not what Red was going for, but she smiled and turned to me with a grin. A second later, I felt a foot running up my leg.

Really? Being questioned about all this was turning her on?

"Well, you all are strange," Sekhmet said, and her head jerked over to Bastet. "No, you wouldn't get to —sorry." After a moment, she said, "Fine, I'll ask. Jack, if we were on the team, would—"

"Not funny," Elisa said, petting Bastet. "Sorry, but you have to break your curse before even getting to talk about this stuff."

Bastet hissed at her and jumped from the table, slinking away.

"She's never been so rejected," Sekhmet said, and then laughed. "We're just fucking with you."

"Wait, now that I think about it," I said, turning to Elisa. "If it's a curse…?"

"A way of breaking it?" Sekhmet asked, guessing where this was going. "We've tried plenty, and at this point Bastet doesn't even want to bother."

"Yeah, but—" I started to protect, only to be shut down by a look from Elisa.

"If you ever want to try, we can," Elisa said. "Breaking curses is one of my specialties."

"I'll be sure to let her know." Sekhmet leaned back, looking me over with a devilish grin. "Seriously, Jack… Jack's ladies. Think about it—one good time with me before I go on my way, after we find your King Arthur, of course."

Elisa smiled kindly and Pucky rolled her eyes, but Red took a moment to look Sekhmet over, while Sharon was merely staring at me, seemingly trying to see what I thought of the whole thing. I stared back.

"It's not weird for you?" she finally asked.

"For me?" I gulped, went for my beer, but she put her hand on it.

"Yeah. While we're on the subject—when I first grabbed you, on the stairs… you didn't resist. Now this—at what point does it become weird for you? Too much?"

I thought about that. I mean really gave the question my attention. "It's already weird, but in a good way. In the way that blows my mind, you know? I have physical limits, I imagine… sure. And emotional."

"And it's like a relationship, but like a team," Elisa said, helping me out. "Right?"

"Exactly." I gave her a nod of appreciation. "I guess that's what helps this feel natural. It's not like we've talked about marriage or anything like that— titles and whatnot, but you're all with me, and I'm this Protector now. Now and forever?" As I said it, my mind started to spin.

"Oh no," Red said, taking Sharon's hand away from my beer and sliding it closer to me. "Don't make him think about it too much, he's going to get scared."

"You've had scared Protectors before?" I asked, then downed the rest of my beer.

Sharon laughed. "I've been responsible for scaring one or two off." At Red's glare, she wiped the smile from her face. "Oh, right… not something to brag about anymore. Sorry."

"Yeah, we've had some quit," Red said, pinching Sharon.

"But you wouldn't do that, would you?" Pucky asked, eyes wide as if that would be something I'd ever consider.

"No," I said, and meant it.

From there, the conversation merged back into recounting the battle we'd just gone through. Basically, we were mentally high fiving each other. We'd earned that and then some. I was glad to have an opportunity to focus on the food, too, and not on my insecurities or discussing our situation. It was what it was—talking about such things only led to confusion and complications.

Whatever the next stage of the journey held, I was going to miss this lamb and—in spite of all of the insanities we'd faced in Egypt, look back on my time there fondly.

15

The plane ride to Milan was, to my relief, uneventful. Well, aside from once being woken from a nap by Sekhmet trying to convince me to join the mile high club. As much as fucking a goddess might have appealed to many a man, I was certainly not lacking in the sex area, nor in the emotional connection area, so politely repeated what the ladies had told her.

If they felt she was ready to join the team at some point, and she accepted, that would be a different story.

At least, that was easy to say when she had her human face on—I couldn't imagine fucking her with the lion face. Sorry, that thought was just too much. It even gave me nightmares, so that when I woke up again it was with the fading image of a lioness tearing into my chest with her teeth as she tried to mount me.

Terrifying.

I looked out the window to see snow-covered mountains, then leaned back and closed my eyes, and focused on my levels and recent upgrades. Just a look for fun, to remind myself how awesome all of this was.

It's possible I drifted off to sleep again after that, but it was sort of a haze. Next thing I knew, I was looking down at the city of Milan as we descended. We kept flying, as apparently we had to land at Malpensa Airport just outside of the city, but had soon landed and found our way to a train that would take us into the city center.

Stepping out into Milan was like finding myself in a mixture of Rodeo Drive in Beverly Hills and some old Renaissance movie about Leonardo da Vinci they'd shown us in my first college art class. First there was the station itself, with its great, curved ceiling of stone and glass, the outside even reminding me of what I thought an ancient castle would look like. Then we were traveling through the streets, walking at first and then taking one of several orange Metro trains we saw screeching around the city.

We exited into the main shopping district and I

was amazed, looking up at the large cathedral while Sekhmet and Bastet worked their tracking magic at our side.

"Duomo di Milano," Elisa said, standing at my side and beaming. "One of the more impressive pieces of architecture still around."

Calling it impressive felt like an understatement. I was left in awe, staring up at its marble spires, with their statues at their tops and gargoyle drainage spouts at the corners. The amount of intricate carvings that went into the designs along the tops of the spires and running along the arches simply astounded me. I couldn't fathom how many hours went into constructing this cathedral that was built in a period of time when modern labor-saving devices weren't available. Everything had been carved by hand. Amazing.

"Is it still used for church services?" I asked.

Elisa smiled and nodded, but then quickly pointed after Sekhmet and Bastet, who had taken the scent and were on the move. Only they paused, turning back.

"What is it?" Red asked.

"The tracking spell isn't perfect," Sekhmet said. "But... we're definitely in the right area."

"So we can't narrow it down further?"

"Unfortunately, no," Sekhmet admitted, while I

took in the giant square, all of the people milling about, and paused, staring up in awe at the golden statue of the Virgin Mary at the top of the cathedral.

"What then?" I asked, not even turning to look at them. All of this was too amazing, and I wanted to capture it, to never forget that I'd been here.

"There's at least one contact here in the city we can call upon," Elisa said. "If he's still around, but I'd be willing to bet he is."

"As long as it's not Heracles," I said, earning an elbow in the ribs from Pucky, though she laughed.

"Not exactly," Elisa said, motioning us on. "Good news though, ladies, we get to pass through some of the shopping area to get to him."

Red rolled her eyes, but Pucky and Sharon both seemed eager.

We stopped at the edge of a wide-open area of this arcaded shopping center, referred to as the Galleria Vittorio Emmanuele II. Here the ground was made up of various mosaics, including a spot where an old lady was spinning on her heel over what looked like a bull. As we got closer, I saw that it was a bull reared up on its hind legs, yellow on a shield of blue.

"They're destroying it," I noted, seeing that the area had been worn down, a bit of a hole even where the bull's testicles would've once been.

"For good luck," Elisa explained.

"Please don't ever step on my balls for good luck."

That earned some chuckles, but Elisa shrugged. "It's the Turin Coat of Arms. Although many don't know where the tradition started… I do."

"And you're going to explain it, I suppose?" Red asked, frowning. Apparently, she wasn't much into this kind of stuff. I was, however, so waited anxiously.

"As a matter of fact, Red, it directly relates to our next move. You see, a Legend named Salvatore—Tore, for short, founded that city as a port to fight against Myths long ago. He actually had grand plans to form an empire, go out and attack humans… but fell in love, instead. It changed him, made him see the error in his ways… and he even went Myth for a while. That is, until she was killed. Ever since, he's been in hiding, to a degree."

"So they stomp on his balls to teach him a lesson?" Sharon asked, chuckling.

"Not stomp, step on and spin. They don't know it, but it's how we would summon him—a man's soul being directly connected to his groin, as we know."

"Um, what?" I asked, but held up a hand. "Never mind, continue."

"Somehow tourists picked up the practice, though for them it doesn't work, of course." Elisa motioned us forward, so that we could take our turn on the bull's balls. "Let's see if it still works for us."

When the old lady and her family in front of us had each had their turn, Elisa smiled and motioned me forward. "Would you like to do the honors?"

"Summon an ancient being by crushing his nuts?" I laughed. "No thanks."

"My cup of tea," Red said, and stepped forward. Grinning at me as she did, she put her heel on the bull's groin and spun. It hurt thinking about it, and I wondered why she was doing that while looking at me. Not cool.

A couple of other tourists passed, smiling at it all, and apparently not noticing the way the tiles of the mosaic started to glow, then ripple across the floor to a corner of the shopping center darker than the rest. They didn't notice the man suddenly standing there, glaring at us, nor the horns on his head.

But we did.

"Looks like it worked," Elisa said, leading us over to him.

He looked furious to have been summoned, and was glancing around, seemingly prepared for some sort of assault or trap. His hair was slicked back between the horns but he wore old sweats, as if he'd likely been relaxing in some hideaway.

"It's been too long, Tore," Elisa said when we stopped a few paces from him.

"Never long enough," he replied. "If I recall, it was your brothers who were to blame for—"

"Don't you dare," Elisa said, quickly closing the gap between them and snatching him by the collar and suddenly seeming to stand over him, tall and imposing. "They sacrificed too much that day, and largely because of you."

"We all have our faults," he snarled, nostrils flaring. "To what do I owe the pleasure?"

"We're looking for someone."

"You know my stance on the war… you know I'm done with it."

"And I know you have a grasp on who comes and goes from this place. King Arthur's here… I want you to tell me where."

Tore didn't show surprise, so I figured he already knew this. He also didn't offer up any information at first, but when he saw Sekhmet step forward, then turned his eyes on me and Excalibur, he arched an eyebrow.

"Arthur, you say?" He grunted. "I don't know about him, but where he goes, you know the Lady won't be far behind."

"The Lady of the Lake," Elisa said, nodding. "Where?"

"Last I heard, there was activity up around Lake Como. Might want to stop bothering me and go find out for yourselves."

"Lake Como it is then." Elisa finally let him go, taking a step back, eyes focused on his. "What aren't you telling us?"

"That you can go fuck yourselves," he said. "Lake Como is where you'll find her, and you know as well as I do she's the key to finding Arthur."

With that he turned counterclockwise and vanished.

"No luck?" I asked.

Elisa grinned at me. "Not from him, not anymore. But at least we have an answer."

"I don't like it," Sekhmet said. "Our tracking is telling us he's here, not... where's this lake?"

"A bit north. Your magic is accurate enough to know he's not there?"

"It is."

"But still, if the Lady of the Lake is..."

"We don't have a choice," Red said.

Elisa nodded, glancing around, taking a moment to look at the nearby shops with their high-end jewelry and clothing.

"It's a shame. I'd hoped to get a chance to upgrade our wardrobes."

Pucky laughed. "There's always tomorrow."

With that, we headed back out of there, making our way for the train station again. Not before, I was relieved to find out, making a stop at a small pizzeria and grabbing some thin slices—as they all were there —to go.

I'll just say this: New York slices had nothing on them.

16

E lisa, not surprisingly, spoke Italian and was able to navigate, along with being able to pull out currency from one of the banks. She gave us each some money, saying it was in case we got split up and there was an emergency.

I loved watching the Italian houses and countryside flash by, with houses built into the hillsides in patches of yellow with red roofs, others out on their own in what was clearly the more luxurious part of the area.

Going through a tunnel, I felt a kiss on my cheek and turned to see Pucky curling up against me. Her arm wrapped around my midsection, and she watched as we exited the tunnel to more hillside beauty.

"Look at our little group, traveling the world together," she said. "Isn't it romantic?"

I was about to agree, but laughed at the thought that it was, in a sense, but the romanticism of it was somewhat offset by the fact that we were hunting evil fairy tales and had fought vampires and worse.

"Something funny?" she asked.

"No, perfect." I kissed her on the top of the head and wrapped an arm around her, sharing a smile with Red, who had taken a seat across from me. The two-hour train ride went by in a flash, and soon we were at the station, ready to see what this place had to offer.

From here it didn't look much different from back home, but with more trees than Southern California, for sure. Lake Como reminded me of Tahoe from back home, with snow-capped peaks in the distance. Several clouds hung over the mountains, but otherwise the sky was completely blue. Fancy villas lined the lake, though from here it was hard to get a good look at them. Maybe one day we'd be able to relax in one of those villas and get a taste for a romantic time that existed long before I was born.

We worked our way down, enjoying the old architecture. An Italian man walked by, singing out loud, and gave us a smile and wave. I was starting to like this place already.

"Have you traveled much?" Elisa asked me.

I laughed. "You mean, aside from Egypt and now Italy? Not at all, really."

"When we have down time, I'll show you the world."

"I'd like that."

"Me too," Sharon said.

"You've not traveled much?"

She shook her head. "I'm fairly new to all this, and they've mostly had me tracking down Myths on America's West Coast, in preparation for a new Protector."

"Very new then," Red said, surprised. "Sorry, I just… I don't know, figured…"

Sharon shrugged. "I'd like to think that, if it were longer, I would've found a way to break free from the shadows long ago."

The only way we could see to get out onto the lake was by the paddleboats shaped as swans. So, going full-on tourist mode—as much to play the part as it made sense on that hot day—we got ourselves gelato and headed out onto the boats. Since it was four to a boat and we had five, Pucky and I took one while the other three ladies took a second. Bastet was deathly afraid of the water and Sekhmet wasn't too fond of it herself, so they found one of the local cafes and agreed to hang out there and wait for us.

They wouldn't be going anywhere, not according to the pact they'd made.

We weren't sure what we were looking for in the lake, only that this was our one connection to the Lady of the Lake that made sense, and therefore it was our best hope of finding Arthur.

At least, that's what the strange bull man had said.

"Can I try yours?" Pucky asked as we paddled out, and held over her sorbet for me to have a lick.

"If you wanted gelato, you should've gotten gelato," I replied, taking a big lick of my pistachio-flavored gelato. "Joking," I added when she pouted, and she took a very seductive lick from the edge of the cone to the top.

"Yummy."

I tried some of her sorbet, and could see how someone would go for it, but not over my pistachio.

"Explain to me again how this works?" I said. "The whole Lady of the Lake thing."

"Hell if I know," Pucky replied, glancing around. "But... lake..."

"That's all you've got?" I laughed.

"I don't always have the answers. I know there was a Lady of the Lake, and I know some of the traditional stories. In some she was with Merlin, gave Arthur Excalibur... stuff like that. But in the real version? Arthur went dark and vanished, Merlin was defeated, and as far as I know the Lady simply vanished. Went into hiding, sick of it all, I imagine."

"Except now that Arthur's back, she's somehow supposed to help us find him."

"They had a strong connection."

"Maybe more?"

Pucky considered this, then nodded. "Likely. It's a similar direction you're headed, Arthur being a Tempest and holding Excalibur meant he had a strong connection with the Fae world. The Lady uses her lakes in a similar fashion, able to travel through them like portals because of her spiritual connection to that place."

We pedaled on for a bit, watching a day cruise out in the distance. I wondered how this all could really be connected. It was so calm, so peaceful out here.

"Ever gotten head on a lake?" Pucky asked, waving over to the other ladies as she steered the boat to face away from them.

"What?" If I'd been taking a drink, I'm sure I would've spat it out. Then again, this kind of talk from Pucky shouldn't have surprised me anymore.

She shrugged. "We're not finding anything out here. We'll probably have to head back, try something else. Might as well get something out of it, no?"

I gulped.

Apparently, there wasn't anything more needed from me to give her the go ahead, because she quickly ducked down, undoing my zipper and pulling out my cock.

"You're kind of a nympho," I said, watching as she slapped my semi-hard cock against her tongue playfully.

"Mmm, proud of it," she replied, and then licked it as she had the gelato. As it grew, she took it in her mouth and moaned.

As fate would have it, that's exactly when a woman emerged behind her, directly into the path of our little swan boat.

"Er, Pucky," I said.

She moaned in response, looking up at me, and froze upon seeing the look in my eyes. Turning slowly, she muttered, "Shit," and quickly tucked my cock back into my pants, as best she could. Women rarely understand how fitting those things in works when erect, so I had to do the rest for her.

Meanwhile, this lady was watching us, simply floating there. Her hair was long and turquoise and floated around her as if it were one with the water. Her eyes blue like the deepest part of the ocean, and skin a slight shade of blue.

"This is how you greet me, Myth?" the lady said,

tilting her head to the side. "With a male's genitals in your mouth?"

"We didn't…" Pucky started, but simply took her seat and frowned, then glanced back to the other boat. I looked too, and saw that they had noticed something was amiss, and were heading our way.

"You were searching for me, no?" the lady asked.

"Again, sorry."

The lady grinned, then shrugged. "We all have our vices, I suppose."

"You are her, no?" Pucky asked. "The Lady of the Lake?"

"That is one of my many names, but I go by Nivian these days," the woman replied, putting up a hand to our boat to stop it from moving. She nodded to the other boat, which was starting to head our way. "Friends?"

"Yes," I replied, and then leaned forward in awe as I noticed a long tail below the surface. The Lady of the Lake was a mermaid!

She, however, thought I was looking at her breasts, it seemed, as she covered them. To be honest, I'd grown so used to my ladies being nude, I hadn't even processed the fact that she was bare-chested. It had helped that her hair was floating around her in the water, providing partial concealment.

"Sorry," I said. "It's just, I've never seen—"

"A pair of perfect breasts?" She eyed Pucky's now, considering. "Seems unlikely."

"A mermaid," I replied.

"He's new?"

"He is." Pucky took my hand in hers, noting that the other boat was coming to a stop slightly behind ours. I was relieved for the help, as this conversation was proving to be very awkward.

As soon as she saw Elisa, Nivian floated away, hands out and wards coming up. "Tore didn't tell me you had a dark one amongst your ranks."

Elisa put a hand on Sharon's shoulder, standing but almost losing her balance. "She's with us now. No longer with them."

"Yet her shadow still lingers," Nivian said, and then turned to me with a hint of scorn. "And now that I realize what it is, I sense it on you, too."

"Who's this, the Little fucking Mermaid?" Sharon shot back, clearly agitated.

"No—" I started, but Nivian shut me off, swimming over to their boat and rising just enough that she looked about to strike Sharon—and enough so that her breasts were now fully exposed, I might add, along with the section at her waist where her skin became glimmering fish scales.

"For a time I was, yes," Nivian said. "And I'd

thank you not to bring up that painful memory. Tell me you were involved so I can gut you here and now."

"Involved?" I whispered to Pucky, very confused by what was happening.

"Nivian's story as the Little Mermaid happened long after Arthur went dark... she fell for Prince Eric, but the Legends got to him after they wed and... destroyed him."

I gulped, seeing how this could be a problem.

To my relief, Sharon shook her head and said, "As a matter of fact, I wasn't even born at that time."

"Not an original?" Nivian said this with almost as much distaste as when addressing her as an enemy, making me like this mermaid that much less.

"There's nothing wrong with that," I said, coming to Sharon's defense. "In fact, in this case I see it as a positive and so should you."

Nivian pursed her lips, lowering herself back into the waters, frowning but seeming to at least concede to my point.

"We're not here to fight," Elisa said.

"No?" I said, suddenly realizing something. "But if we're looking for her, and she's... with Arthur? Wouldn't that make her our enemy?" All eyes went to me. "Well... no?"

"Arthur..." Nivian said, starting to back up, glaring. "Arthur's in a complicated situation. The point is that he's returned to me, and from there I will figure it out. I came here today as a favor to Tore, but really to warn you—back off. Leave Arthur alone, or you answer to me and mine."

"Only problem with that," Pucky said, "he's our only link to finding Morganna."

The mention of the name sent hatred into Nivian's eyes, and she glanced around, then leaned in. "Hear me now—never say her name around me. Arthur is in my care. He will *not* be part of this fight!"

"There's no other way."

"I came here to tell you to leave us be," Nivian said, seething, eyes taking on a darker tone, narrowing, teeth growing sharp. "I came to tell you to get far away from us, to never return—but if you won't listen to reason… You've forced my hand."

A sky that moments ago had been the perfect tourism blue with not a cloud in sight, suddenly transformed to one of swirling black clouds. Nivian dove, waters swirling with her as she moved, so that the surface rocked and sent us back and away.

From the shore came a burst of purple as Sekhmet and Bastet tried to get our attention, but we had enough going on here.

"For one so against the shadows, this feels pretty

fucking dark!" Sharon shouted, eyes flaring red as she worked to fight whatever was going on.

"If she's harboring Arthur…" Elisa started, but cracking thunder cut off her last words.

"She's using the lake as a portal," Pucky shouted from my side, "similar to how witches make portals, but this is different. She's doing it as a Tempest would, and I can sense it on the spirit realm." Pucky took my hand, eyes wide with excitement. "Get to her, grab hold. If you can access your new powers, like we did when making love, we might be able to keep the link open, to follow her."

"How exactly?" I asked, standing and watching as a burst of light swirled below.

"Swim!" Pucky said, and in one quick motion she pulled Excalibur from my side and shoved me into the water.

"No!" Sekhmet's cry carried over faintly from the shore where she stood, but I'd have to find out why later.

I didn't have a choice in this, apparently. I reached out for Nivian as I held my breath, focusing my Fae connection on trying to reach her, to latch onto her. There was no reason to know if it would work or to expect it to, but she was there, cursing me and lashing out with her tail, flying at me with claws at the ready.

My arms sliced through the water and, to my surprise I was thrown out of the way. Right, Tempest! I'd forgotten that my chosen class now had to do with elements, with water being a major part of that. Her eyes went wide with surprise, but that didn't stop her assault. In fact, she smiled, clasping her hands together. The light from below shot up, water swirling around it and coming for me.

Again I threw myself sideways, barely dodging it, but realized what she was doing as the light took one of the boats above—she wasn't going to use this portal or whatever it was she was creating to escape, but to send us away!

To my horror, the boat with Elisa, Red, and Sharon came swirling down with the light. They were scrambling in confusion, trying to reach for me. I threw myself at them this time, but it was no use. Swirling, roaring light shot out long tendrils of luminosity that reminded me of a massive octopus grabbing hold of them... and they were gone.

I screamed, forgetting my need for air, and charged Nivian. If my attack had been against anyone else, it might have worked. But not her—this was her domain. Her tail came up to slam into my back as she changed direction and then came across my midsection, drawing a stream of blood as another swirling light went for Pucky.

No way was I letting it take her too, but without breath, I didn't know what to do. Instead of staying here and trying to fight this mermaid, I shot up for the surface, hoping to grab Pucky and make for shore.

Instead, she went shooting past me, mouth clamped shut and eyes wide with panic, but Excalibur held out for me. I grabbed it and watched her horns glow as she shot past, hoping she would be able to teleport or whatever it was she did. Before she was able, the light took her and she was gone too.

Fuck me.

Almost at the surface, Nivian charged me. I had Excalibur, though, and the sword fueled my powers. Before she could reach me I changed direction, caught her with a good slice to the arm, then went for another strike—fast, direct for her heart. Her only chance was the light, and she took it.

In a flash, she was gone and the waters had returned to normal. I surfaced, spluttering, confused, and glanced around.

It shouldn't have come as a surprise that everyone up here was going about their business, oblivious to what had just happened. Swan boats moved out from the dock, a sailboat in the distance, and tourists were walking about enjoying the sunlight, not a cloud to be seen.

I treaded water, wondering what the hell I was going to do. Finally Sekhmet calling my name got my attention, and I remembered that I wasn't completely alone, at least.

Swimming back to shore, I swore we'd find a way to go after that fucking mermaid, find my team, and get to Arthur. No matter what the cost.

M y return to shore happened in a flash, with Sekhmet helping me out of the water and Bastet pacing, hissing at the lake as if to say she'd been right to hate the water. She had a good point.

"What the fuck do we do now?" I asked, after spewing out the quick version of what had happened.

Sekhmet glared at the lake, chest heaving. "How could you let this happen?"

"Me?" I took an aggressive step toward her, clenching tight to Excalibur. "If you two hadn't been scared of fucking *water*, we wouldn't be having this talk!"

Bastet hissed at me, but Sekhmet held up a hand and said, "No. Turning on each other does no good here. We still owe the price of leading them to Arthur, and…" She eyed me to see if I was catching on. After a moment, she took out her blades and seemed about to cut me, but then ran them over me, flames going just enough to act like a quick-drying spell.

"Since your tracking spell led us to Milan, he can't be far away," I said. "But Nivian—The Lady of the Lake?"

"A distraction."

"Still leaving us with the question of what we're supposed to do now."

"Well, considering someone led us here…" she spun back toward the direction of the station, back to Milan where we'd met Tore, and started walking, Bastet at her heels.

"I'm just supposed to follow you?" I called after her. Seeing people eye me with curiosity, I rolled my eyes and started after her. "Do we have a plan at least? Just go ask him again?"

"This time we're not asking," Sekhmet replied. "We're demanding."

I heaved Excalibur up onto my shoulder, careful not to cut off an ear. "I like the sound of that."

Taking the train back to Milan was painful, in that it took two hours and we knew we were running out of time. Still, our only hope right now was this Tore character. If I thought there was a chance of reopening the portal in the lake, believe me, I would've done it, even if it meant drowning in the process. There wasn't anything I wouldn't do for my ladies.

It went quickly, though, and soon we were back in that shopping district, all of it looking much less glamorous this time around. Sekhmet took the honors of stomping on the character's balls to summon him.

"You?" he said, emerging from the shadows. He stood tall, muscular, his horns glimmering in the sun that shone down from the glass above. "You have no business with me."

He stepped back into the shadows, starting to fade, but Bastet was fast, darting over and encircling him, casting a purple glow upon him that brought him back. Sekhmet closed the distance in three strides, grabbing him by one of his horns and slamming his head into the wall behind, so that it broke the edifice, creating a hole. We followed him through, into a narrow alley. Bastet darted behind us, throwing up another of her purple barriers that, I imagined, made none of this visible.

Sure enough, people kept on walking, nobody paying any attention to us.

"Now," Sekhmet said, still holding Tore by the

horn, one of her curved blades at his neck. "I'm not going to ask nicely this time, because you're standing between me and freedom. Where is Arthur?"

"This isn't my fight, but if you insist on dragging me in, I'll see that you regret it."

"Try your worst." Sekhmet kneed him in the gut and threw him to the ground, and was about to leap on him to show him she meant business, when two wolves darted out, tackling her. Before she hit the ground she was a lioness, Bastet at her side, and the four animals were going at each other.

That left me and Tore, and he was up, starting to run away!

I charged, drawing my sword and shouting for him to stop, only to find three ninjas swooping down. Yeah, fucking ninjas!

"What the fuck fairy tale are you from?" I asked, skidding to a halt and preparing to go up against the closest.

"Fuck you, that's what," that one said, and leaped for me. Thank God, Sekhmet charged in at that moment, plowing through him and giving me room to move to the outside and pursue Tore.

Or so I thought—but as soon as I'd made it two steps, a throwing star lodged in the wall by my head, chipping stone, and then one of the ninjas was charging me with sword held high. Damn, there was no way I was going to be able to stand toe-to-toe in a swordfight against a ninja… but I'd been leveling up and maybe, just maybe, I'd be able to outrun the fucker.

So I ran for Tore, going all out. When I glanced back I saw with relief that Bastet had managed to block off the ninja, and now all three were dealing with Sekhmet, along with the two wolves, and she was holding her own.

Damn, that lady was badass!

But as I moved into the back alley and then turned a corner, the bull of a man plowed into me. His horns caught my arm. They didn't puncture skin, but landed on each side so that Excalibur flew from my grip, clattering to the cobblestone road.

He slammed me against a wall and pulled back, eyes furious, and landed two good punches.

"Our kind aren't involved!" he shouted, then punched me a third time. I thought my ribs were going to break if he got another hit in, so I wrapped my legs around the back of his and threw my weight onto him, taking out his knees. We rolled to the ground and I used what little wrestling they'd taught me to move around to his back and, improvising, grabbed him by the horns, pulling back.

"By fighting us, you've chosen a side," I said, and slammed his face into the ground, hard.

"Fuck you!" he shouted, and then I slammed his face down hard again.

When I pulled him up again, twisting his head by the horns, he held out a hand and said, "The golden statue of the Madonnina."

I glanced around, expecting there to be a Madonna—the singer—statue around, then wanted to slap myself. Of course he meant the statue of the Virgin Mary, the one at the top of the cathedral.

Sekhmet was there in a flash, blade held at Tore's throat. She looked like she'd actually cut him.

"No need," I said to her, releasing Tore. "Arthur's at the Duomo di Milano."

"He said so?" She backed off, standing as Bastet arrived, circling her feet. Behind them, a purple wall of light blocked the others from pursuing.

"But you're likely too late, aren't you?" Tore snorted.

"Meaning what?"

"You've used the sword, no? Not like you did before, I'm guessing, but—to have escaped the Lady, you must have truly called upon its powers. I'm quite certain Morganna will be able to find you now."

"If we discover you've led us astray," Sekhmet said, bringing her blade up to the base of the horn. "I'll have your horns ground up and served in my next soup. Got it?"

He glared, nostrils flaring, but replied, "You'll find him there. It's the only spot she could find that would restrain him.

That gave me pause. Why would she have wanted to restrain Arthur? But Sekhmet released Tore and strode past me, through her sister's spell, and back into the now increasingly crowded throng of people.

I ran to catch up, and when I reached her she started running too, Bastet at her side. We didn't have time to waste, not with my team taken and Morganna likely coming for me next.

"How is he not an enemy at this point?" I asked, trying to understand why he would have led us astray to begin with.

"They follow their own code," Sekhmet said. "I've come across his type in my day—in my mind, it's better to go evil, because then at least we know who to fight. Those like him hide in the shadows and play both sides, when convenient."

"No offense, but—"

"Am I the same?" She scoffed, but her eyes betrayed her uncertainty. Finally, she muttered, "We'll see."

We ran along streets crowded with shoppers and tourists. If I was going to spend my life seeing cities in this way, so be it, but I certainly hoped there'd be some of the more relaxing variety of sightseeing in my not-too-distant future. Making love to these ladies while looking out over the Coliseum in Rome, for one, would be a nice way to spend an afternoon —while not worrying about where our next fight would be.

Then again, all of this action was fun as hell. I kind of liked the high of the fight, the risk of not knowing what was coming next.

We reached the open area with the cathedral, and Sekhmet slowed, considering the high spires and how we were going to reach the top.

"No matter what anyone says, or who stands in our way, no stopping," she said, and kept right on, heading for the doors.

"That's the plan? Just push our way through?"

"Meow," Bastet replied, as if that were the obvious and only choice.

"Worst case, Bastet gives them some illusions to work through." Sekhmet opened the door and we entered. It felt like I'd just walked into an amplified version of the Hogwarts great hall—minus the actual magic stuff. No floating candles or pumpkins or whatever. The ceiling arched up in multiple positions, massive columns with more carvings at their top, and pew after pew arranged to face the front. We turned to the wall to move along the sides, passing various statues and stained-glass windows depicting saints and biblical scenes. I had to ask about it.

"All this... God, the saints...?"

"You're asking if there's a God?" Sekhmet hissed, ignoring the couple walking past and glancing our way only briefly. "How would I know?"

"I just assumed, I mean with the way you all live so long and the spiritual realm and all that—"

"No."

"'No,' as in there's no God?"

She frowned, gave Bastet a look like I was an idiot, and said, "No, as in you assumed wrong. Anyone who claims to know for certain is fooling you—or trying to sell something. Believe if you want. Our existence, the existence of the Fae world and everything that comes with it, none of that has to do with whether there's a one God or not. Believe in what you want to believe in, and don't let outside forces dictate that."

I actually liked that answer, especially in a cathedral as grand as this. That didn't mean I had any idea of what I actually believed, but hearing it from her in this cathedral gave me some relief. If she'd told me a definitive answer one way or the other, I wanted to think I'd still have chosen to make up my own mind on the subject someday, but either way I was content to not know, and to have everything I was doing be unrelated.

It was all too confusing, and right now I simply wanted to focus on getting my ladies back. Oh, and finding Arthur and Morganna so we could kick their asses.

"Hey," my hand reached out for her arm, stopping her, though the slightest touch sent a slight shock through my body that I hadn't been expecting. I dug into my pockets and found some damp euros that Elisa had given me, then pointed to an elevator. "Says it takes us to the top. We just give them some of this."

"I'm familiar with payment systems," Sekhmet said with a sneer, but then smiled. "Good thinking. Much easier than what I had in mind."

We entered the elevators with several other tourists after buying tickets, and were almost to the top when the elevator suddenly stopped, the doors ripped open, and one of the stone gargoyles—now alive with fierce, red eyes, stared right at me.

As much as I'd seen lately, somehow this still gave me the sudden urge to shit myself. To my credit, that didn't happen, but I still felt like a big ol' wuss when I let out a whimper, even as my hand went to Excalibur and I prepared to fight.

It wasn't until then that I noticed that one of the

people in the elevator was a small boy, staring at the gargoyle with as much fright as likely showed on my face. Maybe more.

I had to be brave, for him—though I was slightly bothered by the fact that he could see the monster—so I stepped in front of them, Sekhmet and Bastet already moving, and prepared to face the gargoyle.

W hen a gargoyle with skin like stone comes at you, the best course of action is to run. We did exactly that, only we ran *at* the gargoyle instead of away, as was our way of doing things. Shrieks came from behind us, but aside from the boy who'd clearly seen the gargoyle, the rest of the tourists probably thought the elevator was simply malfunctioning.

They'd be fine, as this monster was after us, not them.

My first blow actually hit, only to be deflected by the strength of the gargoyle's skin. Sekhmet's blades came in fast at my side, diving under my blade as it ricocheted, then coming up with two quick strikes that actually sent the beast stumbling back. As it recovered, I got a good look at the thing—about the size of a large dog, it had a hooked jaw with sharp teeth, wings that spread out behind it in a way that reminded me of a dragon, and sharp claws to match.

"You've got to be fucking kidding me, I said, sooo wishing this was an episode of that amazing *Gargoyles* show that used to be on. Sit me on a couch with a box of Oreos and a liter of Coke any day instead of making me fight one of these things.

Sekhmet and Bastet joined in the fight, charging in with the goddess making several large slits in its stony hide with her fiery blades, and the cat boxing it in with purple light so there was only one direction of attack. We lined up, me with my sword held high, Sekhmet with her blades at the ready, and Bastet hissing and showing her teeth.

The gargoyle flapped its wings and charged us.

"Move!" Sekhmet said, and took a step to her left, away from me. I did the same as she said, "Go for the wings," and we attacked as one. Excalibur sent a crack through the wing on my side while her blades cut the other wing clean off, and then the gargoyle went over the other side of the narrow walkway, trying to flap its wings to get balance, and then desperately trying not to fall. One wing was gone though, so it spun, and then the one I'd damaged broke off.

The gargoyle's expression turned to fear, an

emotion it probably hadn't ever felt before, a second before it fell from sight, shattering far below.

"I thought gargoyles only came to life at night?" I admitted, and she gave me a confused look. "Sorry, too many cartoons." That didn't seem to make it any clearer, so I moved on from the subject.

Or wanted to, but the gargoyles didn't seem to think it was that sort of time, as three more had just clawed their way over the side of the roof.

"Charge through them," Sekhmet said.

"Just... charge?"

She nodded. "Let us handle the rest."

Fuck it, why not? At her nod, I turned and ran, prepared for whatever they'd bring my way. But as I did, each foot founding on that narrow parapet high above Milan on what would've otherwise been a glorious day for standing and staring over the red roofs of this stunning city, the gargoyles seemed confused. They turned and swung at the sky, then one hit the other. When they came at me, it was only to dive for a spot three feet to my rear, followed by a good clobbering from Sekhmet before she and Bastet were coming after me.

"Illusions?" I asked, remembering what we'd faced when first finding Sekhmet.

"My sister's quite good at them, even in cat form," she replied, and then put her blades away and got out the scepter, stopping to shoot a blast back at the pursuing gargoyles with it.

They fell back, and we ran.

We were almost to the base of the spire with the golden Madonnina when a final step sent us through what had been an invisible barrier. As soon as we passed through, gold light shot out, surrounding us, and we found ourselves on another section of the cathedral's roof, an entrance just ahead of us, a bench and some holy water next to it.

No sign of the pursuing gargoyles remained.

"So you've come," a voice said, and I noticed feet from the corner of that entryway, then the man standing. He was regal, to be sure—standing tall, but a look of defeat on his craggy face, a dark shadow hanging over him. While his clothes were those of a great king, red over a white tunic with gold trim, his eyes were red, vampire fangs clearly visible when he spoke. "And led her right to me."

I glanced at Sekhmet in confusion, hoping she had some idea of what was happening, but before either of us could act, one of the women from the elevator laughed, drawing our attention back to the direction she'd come.

"You thought you could hide from me?" she said, transforming into Morganna as she lifted her hands and black, swirling tendrils emerged. The tendrils moved across the golden barrier, so that cracks began to show. "Oh, Arthur, we're connected now."

Arthur let out a roar as the shadows burst in through the barrier, surging around him. Sekhmet and Bastet turned to face Morganna, Sekhmet tucking the scepter away and drawing her blades while I held Excalibur up, not sure which direction to go, trying to look in both directions at the same time. Wasn't Arthur evil and on her side? It seemed there was more to their story than I understood.

But when the shadows hit him, surrounding and engulfing the man, he rose with fangs extending, eyes going red, and turned on me.

He charged, going faster than even Red could move with her cloak—in a flash he had me, head back and fangs about to sink into my neck, when a flash of gold hit and he stumbled back. I fell to my knees in horror, struck with the realization of how close I'd come to death, and turned to see that Sekhmet had managed to lodge one of her blades into Morganna's side, while Bastet was making purple barriers that helped stop the darkness.

"I told you," Sekhmet said with a grin my way as she twirled her second blade, "she's no match for me."

"No," Morganna admitted, pulling the blade free and tossing it to the ground, stumbling as she muttered a spell with a hand over the wound. "I might not be yet, but I soon will be."

Another surge of darkness hit, managing to work around Bastet's barriers, and Arthur was up and charging as he growled like a monster. He wasn't coming for me, though, but running for the edge of the roof. I was about to go after him, but became confused when I saw Morganna leap at the same time as him, the darkness catching both of them and darting about like black lightning in a thunder cloud before folding in on itself and disappearing.

We all stared in dumb shock.

"Arthur...?" a voice said, and a woman came stumbling out of the area he'd first emerged from.

Bastet hissed, instantly on guard, and Sekhmet rolled, recovering her second blade and turning on the woman. Now with legs and fully clothed, it took me a moment to recognize Nivian, the Lady of the Lake. She wore a green dress now, one that clung to her quite nicely, and she no longer looked the part of a monster. Even her skin almost had a normal look to it, her hair seemingly more blonde than blue here.

"You should've gone with your friends," Nivian said, staring at us in horror. "You've doomed him... doomed us all."

"What are you talking about?" I said, lowering my

guard as I realized she wasn't about to attack. "Where are my friends?"

"They're safe, in the spirit realm. But us?" She shook her head in disbelief. "Morganna's going to bring back Merlin and all the power he has, all the power he stole over the ages... and take it for herself."

"We're familiar with the concept," Sekhmet said. "Where?"

"Where else?" Nivian stared at the spot they'd vanished for another long beat, before saying, "The land of magic. The Druids... Stonehenge."

Everyone let that process silently for a long moment before I interrupted by saying, "So... more plane tickets?"

Nivian's eyes flashed to the sword in my hand, then to Sekhmet and Bastet. "I don't think that'll be necessary. Excalibur has a connection to him that will never be broken. Combining that with your tracking and my ability to travel—"

"I don't see any lakes here," Sekhmet pointed out.

"Leave that part to me," Nivian said, gesturing us back over to the bench where Arthur had been standing when we first arrived. She stopped at the bowl of water, and gestured for us to stand at her side. "Holy water—whether there's a direct connection to the heavens or something else, it has a magic to it. A magic that helps me stay like this, versus how I was when we met."

"You mean it fights off the shadows?" I asked, eyeing the water with awe. We'd already faced several instances where that could have come in handy.

"And right now, it's going to serve us in another fashion. You've learned how to harness the blade's magic?"

I frowned. "Maybe? To a degree."

"We'll have to hope that's enough." She turned to Sekhmet. "I've heard enough about you to assume you two set up the tracking spell. It's still in effect?"

After a quick glance at the cat, Sekhmet nodded.

"And my friends?" I asked.

"I'll be able to send you to them after we save Arthur," she replied.

While I had no way of knowing if it was true, I knew it was my best chance at the moment. So when she poured holy water on the blade and told me to focus on the sword and its connection to Arthur as we stood facing each other, I closed my eyes and did as she commanded.

A burst of light flashed and my eyes were open again, our surroundings spinning, becoming a blur, and then, in another flash, we were there—at the outskirts of Stonehenge. Morganna was there with

Arthur, an army of Shades and Legends surrounding us in the dusky evening light. All manner of fairy tales had been gathered for this occasion, I saw— flying monkeys, trolls, witches and spirits. A few celebrities were in the mix, such as a woman with three bears, who I assumed to be Goldilocks; a man with a blue beard, Medusa and several other snake ladies, and even Captain Hook. I wondered how the captain was doing without Pan around.

Morganna had Arthur on his knees, leering at him.

Morganna's eyes slowly rose to meet ours, and she laughed. "Isn't this cute? You came to witness my victory." Turning to the kneeling Arthur, she waved her hand our way and said, "Give the rest of our visitors a show, while I finish the ritual."

Arthur spun on us, and this wasn't the same Arthur we'd seen at the top of the Milan cathedral. He wore the same clothes and had the same look, but his red, glowing eyes showed the ferocity of a demon. When he came at us, fangs extended and claws at the ready, I had no idea what I was supposed to do. It wasn't like I could just let him suck my blood, but we couldn't really kill him either.

Sekhmet charged in with Bastet at her side, and I saw for the first time how truly dangerous they could be. Bastet was darting around, leaping and changing directions as she created patterns of purple light that worked to contain Arthur's movements. While he was fast, if he was suddenly blocked in his direction, then blocked in his next move, speed didn't do much for him. And in the meantime, Sekhmet had her scepter in her hand again and opted for it here over her blades in a way that sent streams of flame at him. Neither, I saw, was working to kill him, but to contain him while Nivian shouted for me to get in at him with the sword.

The Legends crowded in, some flying overhead, clearly wanting a piece of the action. I tried to keep an eye on them, waiting for the moment that Morganna gave them all the go ahead to charge in.

At the moment, however, Arthur was keeping us busy. I was finally close enough and deflected a blow with my newly-upgraded shield, while Nivian called to him in one breath and then shouted for me to strike him with her next.

"Won't it kill him?" I shouted back, narrowly avoiding a strike from his long claws as Sekhmet pounced on him in her lion form and then rolled off, shooting flames that nearly took him. She lifted the scepter and the flames arched, so that Bastet could, instead, dive in and again block off Arthur.

"The blade still has the magic of the holy water," she said. "Strike him, but not lethally."

"Great, make it easy next time," I countered, again charging in. My Tempest tattoos were glowing, going crazy as they swirled across my skin, and the power within me was surging in response.

A purple wall of light faded and Arthur was roaring as he leaped for me, but I managed a burst of speed, ducking under and slicing—and sure enough, the sword tasted flesh.

It hit him in the side, coming out with a spurt of black blood.

But when Arthur turned to me, the red glow from his eyes was fading even as the wound healed itself.

"Thank you," he mouthed.

We weren't given time to celebrate our victory, because Morganna had risen into the air, gowns fluttering in the wind as clouds rolled past. She shouted, "That was growing dull, at any rate. Let us get on with it."

Then, bringing her hands together, the clouds above erupted in bursts of lightning and one shot down, straight into Arthur, so that he was stuck in place, the light too bright to see what was happening, while Morganna's mad laughter filled the air.

Cheers erupted from her gathered Legends.

"Do something!" Nivian screamed, for the first time apparently not having answers.

Sekhmet changed her fire attack to Morganna, but the latter threw up a hand that created an emptiness where the fire vanished.

"You fools," Morganna said, floating over to the center of the standing stones, a jerk of her hand causing Arthur to fly out of the lightning and land next to her. "Didn't you know that by the time you got here, it was already too late? The second *we* arrived here, it would've been too late."

I tried charging, but a burst of energy shot out from the stones, knocking me and my companions back.

"Go ahead, get rid of them," Morganna said to her horde. As the enemy started to close in on us, she muttered a chant, hands lifted to the sky, and more magic flowed out of the gigantic standing stones.

The first to reach us, as we were recovering and getting to our feet, were the flying monkeys and those who could move in bursts of magic, like the witches. If not for Bastet's magic I would've been toast in seconds. She and Sekhmet were both damn powerful, and Nivian began to get more involved too, muttering chants that acted as buffers and enhancers. When I lunged for a counterattack against three trolls, the sword felt like a toy as I cut through them, moving faster than I was pretty sure Mr. Vampire Arthur himself had.

A claw snagged me and yanked me back, throwing me to my ass. I lifted my arm so that my shield appeared to block as a sword came down, and when I looked up I saw Hook there, sneering at me.

"The man who killed Peter Pan," Hook said, and laughed. "You'd think I'd be thanking you."

"You still can," I said, realizing it had been a hook that had yanked me down, not a claw.

"Not likely," he replied and came back with a strike from his hook and then his sword, the later catching the side of my arm but only with a slight cut.

"See, after all these years I was growing rather fond of the lad," Hook said, trying again as I rolled aside and recovered. He squared off against me, the two of us going blow for blow. "I even liked him bossing me around. Poor form, perhaps, but jolly good fun."

"You're fucked," I replied, coming in for a strike, "in the head."

"Ah-ha." He blocked the blow and came in for an uppercut strike with his hook, pulling blood from my chin but not landing in my neck as he'd attempted. "So you *do* get me."

"I get that you're about to meet your maker, fucking pirate." I lunged and struck, but only as a feint before kicking out one of his legs and bashing him with the pommel of my sword. For some reason, killing the good ol' captain felt wrong, so I left him there, moaning in pain, and turned to face my next opponent.

There were plenty left to keep me occupied.

More enemies and Shades kept coming, and my levels started stacking on top of each other to the point that I think I leveled up to twelve. I was pretty sure I'd gotten an Ichor or two along the way as well.

All the while we were trying to reach the standing stones, but couldn't quite make it. Bursts of light and darkness, explosions and what looked like opening rifts formed and surrounded the sky above the stones, until three flying monkeys were sucked in and a couple of witches. The rest started steering clear of it, some even forgetting to fight, simply focusing on trying to escape this force that was acting like a magnet, pulling those nearby into it.

And then, as Morganna lifted Arthur to her and pressed her lips to his—almost like in the fairy tales, but in a much darker, twisted turn of events—he turned to ash in her grip, floating up and into the void she had created.

The last of him entered, and then it collapsed in

on itself with a burst of red light that shot outward, knocking us all over and pausing the fight.

When I looked up again, all of the void and the storm was gone, replaced by a single man who was standing there with his long white robes flowing, a beard of white and grey to match.

"Merlin," Morganna said, smiling wickedly.

"You," he replied in a raspy voice, moving his hands to form a spell, but she simply stepped forward before he could finish and thrust her hand onto his heart. It was as easy as that—no magic, no fight to the death. She pulled her hand back, and with it the glowing red Ichor I'd come to recognize, as Merlin's body collapsed to the ground where Arthur's should have been.

Morganna absorbed the Ichor, and before our eyes she seemed to grow in size and power. It was like a shadow had fallen over her, but her eyes glowed bright green and the air around her seemed to push outward, as if she had too much power and it was taking up all of that space.

We had failed—Morganna had won.

20

My first thought was to run in and attack, and believe me—I tried. With all of the buffers from Nivian, along with my magic shield and enhanced sword, I actually believed I had a shot. Charging at her with Excalibur held high, blue was trailing me and my skin was crawling with the power of my tattoos feeding me more energy. My war cry would've scared the largest grizzly bear, maybe even a dragon, I was certain.

And yet, all it took from her was a swipe of her hand to send a gust of wind at me that threw me back and onto my ass. With another swipe, a burst of lightning shot out and nearly hit me, but I held up Excalibur and the lightning hit, surging through me in a way that actually gave me *more* power! This was the first time I'd seen that skill class upgrade come into effect, and I was impressed.

I thrust forward with the sword and watched with excitement as the blast of lightning went right back at her. She held up both hands in annoyance, causing the lightning to bounce off of her. At least it took out a goblin and sent Captain Hook, who had just recovered, stumbling back, his hair smoldering and eyes looking dazed.

An explosion sounded and I turned to see Morganna looking dazed, but pissed. Sekhmet was there, scepter in hand, grinning. With her at the reins, I took the opportunity to upgrade as fast as I could—I'd need everything I could get. A quick upgrade to the shield that would send a shield stun out and then I paused, grinning. My group Tempest attack was ready, and I had the Ichor point!

It was mine, and now I couldn't wait to try it out.

Morganna and Sekhmet were facing off, all hell about to break loose.

"You want a plaything, is that it?" Morganna said to Sekhmet with a sneer. "See, I'm too busy for you... so let's see if your friends can come out to play."

None of us knew what she was talking about, I was sure, until she brought up one hand and one of the massive standing stones fell backwards, breaking the ground around it. A moment later, hands

reached up, pushing dirt aside, and I expected skeletons or zombies to come stumbling out.

Instead, it was our enemy from the tombs, Isis
herself. She wasn't alone, however. Crawling out at
her side and then standing tall with a roar of exalta-
tion to be free was a man I hadn't seen before, but
one who wore Egyptian robes and had bursts of
silver and black coming out of him like twisting
light.

Sekhmet took a step back, fell to one knee, and
her mouth hung open. Apparently, this man was the
last person she wanted to see right now. It was Ptah,
her former lover who had deserted her for Isis. All
this time Sekhmet had guarded against this moment,
and now he was free to do his worst again, thanks to
Morganna.

"Enjoy the gift," Morganna cackled, returning to
her magic to attack me as I charged again. At least I
was putting up a bit of a fight, now that I knew I
could absorb certain Tempest spells and use the
sword to shoot them back, even if it was only hitting
the surrounding monsters and distracting her.

Two large lizards came up from my rear while a
small man with a crooked nose—Rumpelstiltskin,
maybe?—leaped at me with a dagger, but I was
charged up and spun on them, cutting through one
lizard and sending blasts of icy wind at the others.

While the small man was preparing another attack, three Shades emerged from his shadow and came at me, but I struck them down with Excalibur boosting out, expanding and shining double. I took the prana while he stumbled back, weakened.

Right now, I didn't see the point in leaving the Legends alive. Too much was at stake. So as much as they'd warned me against it, I charged the man and removed his head with an amplified, clean strike, absorbing his Ichor a moment later. Bam—level thirteen, and I had an Ichor to use.

"Be careful!" Sekhmet shouted as she came to my side, and I almost snapped back at her. She saw the look in my eyes, and pointed at Isis and the man. "They're our enemies here. You defeat, you capture —kill if you have to—but remember that every life you take by choice, rather than because you're left without any other option, affects you, breaks down your resolve to fight the shadow.

She was right, of course. I was already feeling like an ass, like an ass who wanted to take more lives and do nasty things. Note to self—killing, bad. Stop it.

Isis roared with laughter, flying at me with her claws at the ready, and the man darted forward in bursts that reminded me of horror movies from the nineties. Luckily for me, Sekhmet, Bastet and Nivian were with me, the four of us going back-to-back in a loose square as the enemies closed around us. The biggest threat seemed to be this new couple, although we still had to deal with the easier foes.

Bastet was weaving purple shields and clawing away like a champion, and my tattoos and Excalibur were in full blue flame mode, bursts like electricity even running up the sword and sending an extra oomph into each strike.

Blast after blast suddenly shot out from Sekhmet's scepter, but they seemed to be missing something, as if she couldn't fully commit to striking down this man. Of course, he had once been everything to her, by my understanding, so it would have to be one of us who dealt the final blow.

He flashed over to her and held out his hands, darkness channeling through him and toward her, so that she fell to her knees, screaming, and the scepter started to slip from her hands. Bastet came to her rescue, the cat darting between Sekhmet's legs and leaping to get a good set of claws dug into the man's groin—he fell back, cursing, trying to swat her off.

Meanwhile I was trying to work toward them, using my new group attack in ways that were blowing my mind. If I thrust into the air focusing on the attack, bursts of electricity shot out, hitting surrounding enemies. A good thrust into the ground would send a shockwave like tremors through the earth, knocking them down. I couldn't wait to see what would happen around water or other elements. Still, I wasn't getting there fast enough.

The man was almost up when I got a lucky shot, boosted by Nivian, that blasted him in the face. With his power, the blast didn't do lasting damage but sent him back on his ass. Bastet rolled out of the way as Isis came at her, but instead of attacking, knelt at the man's side and cradled his head, checking on him.

I had a feeling the relationship between these four had been a complicated one. A story for another day, because everyone seemed to have stopped fighting then, as something in the sky seemed very out of place.

A helicopter was coming right for us.

We all stared, dumbfounded, watching it land. I expected Morganna to hit it out of the air with one of her spells, but she stood there watching like the rest of us. She must've been equally as confused, though, because she simply took a step toward it, hair not even reacting to the wind from the blades, and stared in annoyance and curiosity.

When the blades stopped and the door opened, out stepped Agent Torrind.

"You look different, Riak," he said, his voice

cutting though the silence. "And look at this mess you've gotten yourself into. But don't worry, Daddy's home."

"Go fuck yourself," Morganna said, and thrust out a hand that sent a barrage of lightning and fire at him, each strike coming one after another in successive hits so that, by the time she stopped, a wall of smoke remained. She chuckled to herself as it cleared, and we saw scorched earth, an utterly destroyed helicopter, and… the agent.

"How…?" Sekhmet said, stepping up to my side, her lioness face contorting in confusion.

I imagine every single person or fairy tale there was asking themselves that exact question.

And Agent Torrind, for his part, had an answer. He held out his hands, his suit destroyed and falling off of him—but his body transformed as it did, so that he was glowing, too bright to look directly at, and began walking toward Morganna.

"You see," his voice came with a hint of familiarity, but much deeper, much more… godly, "we didn't allow you to run unchecked all these years simply because humans were stupid enough to believe you'd help them win the war against fairy tales. No—while they are that stupid, you were left alive because of me. You were chosen to lead me here, to finally achieve your destiny, your calling."

"And that is?" Morganna asked, voice starting to show worry as it cracked.

"To allow me out of my cage," he replied, and in that second the light faded as his head transformed into that of a falcon one minute, a strong man with fiery hair the next.

"Father," Sekhmet muttered, eyes wide. Her hand took my arm and she whispered, "We have to go... now."

"Go where?" I hissed, and saw that Nivian was inching closer to us, Bastet at my feet.

"Anywhere but here," Sekhmet muttered. "Now."

"Father...?" I said, putting this together. "You mean that's—"

"Ra. Yes. Now, can we...?"

"Ah, daughter," Ra said, eyes turning to us with a hint of humor. "I'll deal with you in a minute, but first."

He suddenly burst forward like a flash of light, hands on Morganna as we'd seen her with Merlin, and while Nivian grabbed me and Sekhmet, Bastet leaping into her sister's arms, we witnessed Ra pulling the Ichor from Morganna, tearing away her magic, her power... her life.

And as his eyes were moving back toward us, Nivian muttered, "Arthur, take us with you!"

I was confused, at first, but then saw what resembled ashes, only sparkling, tumbling down from the sky, falling around us. Our surroundings started to fade as Ra began to address his new followers.

"You have a choice," he said. "You now follow me, or die. And when I say die, I mean completely—there will be no prisoners under my new world order. The gods have returned, and we *will* control this world along with all others."

He kept on, but his voice became muffled, the last bit barely audible as he seemed to have noticed us vanishing and began commanding the others nearby to stop us from escaping, kill us or die themselves.

I might have felt bad for them, if not for the fact that they'd been trying to kill us moments earlier. What was happening with us, though, I had no idea.

We seemed to still be alive, floating in grey mists. Nivian was to my right, eyes wide, searching, while Sekhmet was holding onto Bastet, both floating to my left. We'd escaped. Our enemies couldn't get to us. For now, at least, that would have to do.

21

My feet were suddenly on solid ground, without falling or even stumbling. Green grass under my feet, the tendrils of mist floating amongst it in patches, rising up in others and even starting to fade. More of what appeared to be a grass field became visible, then several weeping willows, and finally patches of blue sky.

By the time it had all faded, I'd had enough time to realize what had happened—that we'd gone through a portal.

"Where'd the portal take us?" I asked.

"Wrong question," Nivian said.

I frowned, realizing I was somehow wrong. "The right one being?"

"You might ask where Arthur took us, and the answer would be that we're in the Fae land."

"Wait a minute," Sekhmet said, letting Bastet jump out of her arms and investigate our surroundings. "Is Arthur not dead?"

"She 'sacrificed' him to call upon Merlin," Nivian answered. "But didn't take his Ichor, didn't end his life, exactly."

"Making that a... I ran a hand through my hair, trying to grasp all of this. "And now we're in Fae land."

"And if we can find the nearest lake..." Nivian turned at a meow from Bastet, where she was already moving off from us toward a lake. In spite of Nivian's weary expression, she actually managed a smile. "There we go."

"How does this help us?" I asked. "I get it out there, but in here?"

"In here, in some senses, works a lot like out there. Our magic can be amplified, in certain ways, and there are, of course, the Fae and the Shades to worry about. As for how this, in particular, will help... Well, watch and learn."

We reached the edge of the lake and she gestured me forward, to look into the water from the edge. I expected her to shove me in or something, so knelt hesitantly, but when I saw my reflection my heart leaped with excitement—there in the reflection, staring back at me, were Red, Sharon, Elisa, and Pucky!

Arms wrapped around me and I turned to see Pucky there by my side, the others now with us too.

"Magic," Nivian explained with a wink. "This is where my darker self sent them... And again, sorry about that."

"She's on our side now?" Red asked, staring at Nivian with hesitation.

"In a strange way, she never wasn't," I replied. "Just, you know..."

"Shadow," Sharon said, nodding.

"That and a desire to protect Arthur," Nivian replied, as she stepped forward and introduced herself, embracing each of them as she apologized. "Not every day you get attacked by a mermaid and sent to the Fae land, is it?"

"Not most days," Elisa replied with a laugh, accepting the hug with grace.

When they were done, Sekhmet cleared her throat, motioning at our surroundings. "So... what now? How do we get back?"

"Honestly, I don't know," Nivian replied. "It was only because of the shadow part of me that I was able to send you here in the first place. Not a power

I'm able to recall without it—and that's not something I'm able to use at will."

"So we're fucked," Red said. "Wonderful.

"I don't get it," I admitted. "This place, it's like a
whole actual world? Not just the strange planes of
mist and Shades I saw with Riak?"

"In a sense," Nivian replied. "It's like this—it was
a land of magic, of fairies, dragons, and more… until
we discovered it. Now there are communities here,
established by fairy tales who no longer wanted to
live among the Normies of Earth."

"So the legends of Arthur going off to live in
Avalon…?"

She nodded. "True, though they left out the
vampire part. At the time, it was one of the only
ways to keep the vampire side of him at bay. To
ensure he no longer faced the darkness, he came
here with me and we enjoyed a long, healthy time
together. That all ended the day he was brought
back."

"I'm so sorry," I said, my heart aching for her.

She bit her lip, nodded, and said, "Come, I'll show
you where we stayed. Maybe he'll be there."

The home she led us to was tucked away behind
trees and up against a cliff-face at the side of one of
many rolling hills. It wasn't horribly constructed, but
clearly had been done without a construction team

in place. The place's saving grace was that it had been nicely decorated with flowers and was surrounded by a garden with all manner of vegetables and fruits growing. I saw one strawberry bigger than an apple, and was willing to bet it was the juiciest, sweetest strawberry I'd ever come across.

"Arthur," she called out, running in, and when I took a step to follow, Elisa put a hand on my arm and shook her head slightly.

We waited while Nivian called out his name several more times, appearing at different windows. After a few minutes, the situation became clear.

She stumbled back, eyes full of sorrow. "I was afraid of this…"

"Could he be… out?" I asked.

"When she sacrificed him like that, she sent him here… in exchange for Merlin, but in a way that didn't leave him whole. He might be here in spirit, but not beyond that." She took a deep breath, processing this, and then tried to smile. "Come, rest. We'll find a way back to the fight when we're all… ready."

The last word had been hard to get out as she tried to stay strong, and then she turned and led us to a room that could be ours. There were only two rooms in the place, and she said she'd work on figuring out more of a bedding situation. Maybe go visit others she knew who came here occasionally, or maybe the Fae would bless us.

She left us to it, and we milled about the room, making ourselves at home. I stared out the window, taking in this world in the glory that it was without the mists, now noticing the hills and mountains in the distance. We had no idea how we were getting out of here, yet, though we were working on it. For now we had accept that as enough, and be happy that at least we were together.

And that meant all the difference—because being together meant we could actually be *together*.

Still, it was frustrating as hell. When Sekhmet, Bastet and I had filled in the rest of the team about what had happened, and we'd discussed our options and decided there really weren't any, I laid back on the bed, closed my eyes, and said, "Fuck."

"I know I'm usually the pessimist," Red said, coming over to me, lying down on the bed next to me, propped up on one arm so that she could look me into my eyes. "But today, no. We've come too far, made too much progress… and the world faces too great of a threat for us to lose hope."

"You sound like a fucking superhero movie," I said, rolling my eyes.

She leaned in, pressed her lips to mine, and said, "That was to make you shut up." I opened my mouth to try and say something else, when she leaned in again for another kiss.

"And that one?" I asked dreamily as she pulled back a tad.

"That was for motivation, inspiration." She gave me a peck, throwing one leg over mine, so that her thigh was pressed against my crotch. "And this one's to get you in that 'superhero' mode, so that when we're done you'll jump up all inspired like you always are, ready to kick some ass."

I was skeptical, considering our situation, but when her lips pressed against mine and our tongues met in a dance of rising passion, I started to see how she made a lot of sense. We were together. We weren't exactly dead—which meant we stood a chance.

The pressure in my crotch told me I was really getting into this, and she must've felt it too, because a second later she had her hand where her thigh had been, caressing my cock through my pants.

"I could use some motivation," Sharon admitted, and she joined us, kissing first Red, then me.

"Should we… leave?" Sekhmet said, her face transforming to that of a woman instead of the lion. "Or stay?"

Elisa and Pucky shared a look, then looked towards Red and Sharon.

"I don't… know," Pucky said. She looked at me. "I suppose it's up to him, since none of us seem to have a problem with it."

"I vote for stay," Sharon said. "More the merrier."

"Oh, I didn't mean…" Sekhmet laughed, nervously. "I didn't mean join in. Sorry, I can see how… yeah… Not yet, at least. Just—do you want privacy? I'll give you privacy. Unless… you like people watching? Where I come from, at least in the circles I ran, it was normal."

More looks at me, and I shrugged. "Sure…?"

Sekhmet smiled, though tried to look like she didn't care one way or the other, and Bastet purred, curling up on her lap.

"Whatever, you all are weird," Red said, turning back to me. "Just don't clap or cheer us on or anything."

A couple of chuckles went around the room, but my mouth was interlocked with Red's again, and my attention on her breasts, which were pressed against me. Her lips were soft, subtle, and couldn't get enough of me. As we kissed, her hands found my clothes and tore them off. My eyes opened and darted over to Sekhmet, but she was standing there with her human face and a smile on her lips.

The cat sat on her lap, purring.

"So… weird," Red said, following my glance.

I flipped her over so she wouldn't see it, though that put my ass and balls in view. That was no good, so I turned instead, flipping her over doggy-style and pulled her skirt up, her panties off.

Then I paused, forgetting that we hadn't taken this step. Her hand, however, reached down and grabbed my cock, guiding it to where it was pressed against her warm, wet pussy.

"Are you sure?" I asked.

She glanced back, bit her lip, and nodded. The others were watching, impressed, not making a move to join, and I supposed they wanted to let it happen this way. To make it special, just me and her... with them watching.

As odd as that was, it was also hot. I let her guide it in, and soon we were rocking that place. She flipped me over and took me at the edge of the bed, riding me. My hands were all over her, grabbing her ass and breasts, feeling at one with her as we finally made it happen.

When she clenched me close, rolling us over so I was on top, she moaned long and low and then released.

She smiled up at me, glanced down to where I was still inside her and said, "Hot damn." Motioning to the others, she said, "Get in there."

Now the other three were moving in, stripping

and caressing me, loving it. Sharon came next, and then I had Pucky riding me, Elisa caressing her back as she kissed me, touching herself. Pucky's breasts were rocking, my body arching as that moment took me.

As I came, my body lit up like it had before. Unlike last time, though, now there were blue flames shooting out from me in bursts, as if I were a blue sun and solar flares were erupting. Fuck it felt good, like I was ejaculating from every inch of my body... as disgusting as that sounds after the fact.

But there was more to it. Pucky was yelping and then saying, "Yes, yes," and at first I thought it was all about the sex, but when I finally finished, I saw it hadn't been. Those bursts hadn't been random light shows or fireworks. Judging by the way they were still shooting off of me, some blue flames now hovering out there, shifting into shapes like little people—what I guessed to be Fae, or some form of them, anyway—I had connected with this place on a whole other level.

And when I heard Elisa gasp as she covered herself with a shirt, I turned to the door to see a body materializing there, forming from bits of blue sparks that were drifting over.

Not a random form, nor a form with characteristics that I couldn't make out, but the very distinct form of Arthur.

When it was done, he stood there looking very much like the real version of him had, only with a blue glow that surrounded him entirely. His eyes, too, were glowing bright blue.

"Thank you, Jack," he said, nodding to me and then averting his gaze. "Please, dress. Bring Excalibur."

"I'm sorry?" I said as he turned to go.

"You're coming with me," he said, not even stopping. "It's time to begin your training."

THE END

Jamie Hawke

After working on Marvel properties and traveling the world, Jamie Hawke decided to settle down and write fun, quirky, and sexy pulp science fiction and superhero books. Are they all harem? Oh yeah. Oh yeahhhh.

It all started when Jamie was eleven, creating nude superhero comics with his best friend. What perverts! But hey, they were fun and provided good fodder for jokes up into their adult years. Now the stories have evolved, but they capture that same level of fun. Hopefully you will enjoy them as much as the author loved writing them!

I had a lot of fun writing this second book in the series, and hope you had as much fun reading the book!

What did you think? More chaotic – in a good or bad way? I enjoyed bringing the Egyptian characters into the story, and gods in general, even if they aren't exactly fairy tales. In a sense, how's it different? They're still stories, but it so happens that at one point there was a culture that thought of these characters as gods. Some people still do, for all I know. But for this story, I thought making them on practically equal footing with the other fairy tales would be more fun.

What started as a contained story in Southern California has now expanded out to Egypt and other parts of the world. Maybe this is why it took me almost twice as long to write this book as it usually does. I had to think about what story threads made sense from the first, make sure I was following through on them, but also consider these various locations and do some research. While I've lived in some of these places, the details don't always stay the same in my mind as they actually were, I learned. Funny how time away from a place does that.

I'm really excited for book three, because they got to go into the Fae land, or spirit realm. But before that, I've promised my readers Supers - Ex Heroes 4 and a prequel to the Supers books that focuses specifically on the fox-lady Charm.

READ NEXT

Thank you for reading MYTH PROTECTOR! Please consider laving a review on Amazon and Goodreads. And don't miss out on the newsletter:

SIGN UP HERE

***

Don't miss the bestseller SUPERS: EX HEROES.

Super powers. Super harem. Super awesome.

Contains Adult Content. Seriously.

Who in their right mind tells both his lawyer and the judge presiding over his murder trial, "Fuck you!" while still in the courtroom? No one, right? Yeah, you'd be wrong about that. I did.

You'd say the same thing if you were just found guilty of a murder you didn't commit, though. Call me crazy for going off like that in court, but trust me, you don't know crazy until you see what happened next.

I never believed in superheroes. I certainly didn't believe that I'd become one, or that strategically forming a harem of hot chicas and getting down with them to unlock my superpowers would be the key to my survival.

Did I say my survival? I meant the universe's. No, really...that's exactly what happened when I was taken to a galaxy of supers, thrown into a prison ship full of villains, and told it was up to me to stop them all.

Read on, friend, because it gets a whole hell of a lot crazier from here.

***

Want something a bit more insane? Planet Kill is like Battle Royale on a planet with Gamelit elements... and it's crazy. You'll see - You can grab book one and two on Amazon!

Grab PLANET KILL now!

Form your harem. Kill or be killed. Level up and loot. Welcome to Planet Kill.

Pierce has his mission: survive by killing and getting nasty, doing whatever it takes to find his lost wife and others who were abducted and forced to participate in the barbarity that is Planet Kill. In a galaxy where the only way to rise up in society and make it to the paradise planets is through this insanity, he will be up against the most desperate, the most ruthless, and the sexiest fighters alive.

Because it's not just a planet--it's the highest rated show around. Contestants level up for kills, get paid for accepting violent and sexual bids, and factions have been made in the form of harems.

His plan starts to come together when he meets Letha, one of the most experienced warlords on the planet. She's as lethal as they come and a thousand times as sexy. He's able to learn under her, to start to form his own harem.

Only, being her ally means fighting her wars.

It's kill or be killed, level up fast and put on the show the viewers want all while proving to Letha and her generals that he has what it takes to be one of them. The alternative is death, leaving his wife to her fate of being hunted by monsters.

CPSIA information can be obtained
at www.ICGtesting.com
Printed in the USA
LVHW110213051118
595963LV00001B/4/P

9 781729 625910